Will the REAL   Please STAND UP?

Julia Lee

Julia Lee

Cold Tree Press
Nashville, Tennessee

Library of Congress Number: 2007937728

Published in the United States by Cold Tree Press
Nashville, Tennessee
www.coldtreepress.com

This book may not be reproduced in any form without express written permission.
Printed in the United States of America
ISBN 978-1-58385-202-6

Dedication

This book is for Bruce, Leah, Katy, Patrick, and Gus.

Acknowledgement

I would like to thank Chris Fletcher, editor of *The Daily Herald* in Columbia, Tennessee, for publishing "The Anonymous Mother."

In addition, I would like to thank Kathy Rhodes, editor of the book *Muscadine Lines: A Southern Anthology,* and *Muscadine Lines: A Southern Journal,* for publishing my writing. I would also like to thank Bob Duncan; Maury County Historian, and Sheila Hickman, Editor of The Maury County Archives Committee, for including me in their publications.

Table of Contents

PART I
MEN AND OTHER MYSTERIES

PART II
FAMILY: THE COLD HARD TRUTH

PART III
NOSTALGIA: RUNNING WITH SCISSORS DOWN MEMORY LANE

PART IV
GIMME THAT OLD TIME RELIGION

PART V
THE FACTS ON HOLIDAYS AND SEASONS

PART VI
GOULASH

Will the REAL ANONYMOUS MOTHER Please STAND UP?

Julia Lee

PART i

Men and Other Mysteries

1. My Monkey

 uman unconditional love exists only between parent and child; namely, mother and child.

Husbands and wives do not love unconditionally.

Siblings do not love unconditionally.

Friends do not love unconditionally.

Employers and employees do not love unconditionally.

I know this on a rational level. Emotionally, it's another story. It seems I believe my husband should love me unconditionally, even if I am not willing to reciprocate. This is a flaw in my personality, and I fear it is here to stay.

Exactly one week ago, we were sitting on the couch, watching monkeys on the Discovery Channel.

"I want a monkey," I said. "They're so adorable."

"I hate monkeys," he said. "Besides, we have children. That's enough."

"But monkeys are so cute! They can learn sign language, and they can be potty trained. I'd just love to hold a little monkey and feel its arms wrapped around me. I could get it a pacifier and feed it a bottle. Wouldn't that be fun?"

"Monkeys scratch, bitc, and mess all over the place," he said. "I hate them."

"You're such a fuddy-duddy!" I said. "Besides, I don't need you to tell me whether I can get a monkey or not. I'll get a kangaroo if I feel like it."

"You get a monkey, and I'm out of here," my husband replied.

I stared at him in disbelief. "You're what?" I asked. "Do you mean to tell me that if I went out and bought a monkey tomorrow, you'd jump ship?"

"Yep," he said.

"What about the kids? Would you abandon your children simply because their mother fell in love with a monkey? What's the matter with you? Lots of people own monkeys. I might even own a monkey someday."

"If a spouse goes out and intentionally does something that her mate strongly disapproves of," he said, picking his teeth with a fork prong, "that's grounds for bye-bye."

"You are heartless! What ever happened to unconditional love?" I screamed.

"Would you stay with me if I roasted your monkey and ate it for supper?" he asked, smacking his lips.

"Of course not, "I said. "I have certain standards."

"Well, it's me or the monkey," he said, shoveling a peanut into his mouth.

"You don't love me!" I cried. Even though I recognized the early stages of PMS, I continued. "If you loved me, I could keep you and the monkey! You make me sick! I'm going to get a monkey!"

"Go ahead," he smiled.

Later that evening, we made up and laughed about our monkey fight. How could we have been so childish? I flicked the remote, and there on the screen was the cutest monkey I'd ever seen. Her name was Daisy, and she was stirring cookie dough and wearing a yellow apron. I turned the off the TV and rolled over, feeling somewhat bruised.

The following night, I turned on the TV, and there sat a handsome monkey named Ralph. He had on a tuxedo, and was playing chess with his girlfriend, Miss Bliss.

"Oh," I cried. "Isn't that adorable?"

"What is this?" My husband said. "Monkey week?"

I think God was trying to get my husband, and I think it was working. I smiled and turned off the TV.

The next night, there was an old mama monkey, standing on a mountaintop. Nature had taken its toll on her breasts.

"Do you think monkeys ever wear bras?" I asked my husband. "If I had a monkey, I would buy her some underwear from Victoria's Secret. Bet you'd like that."

My husband laughed. "You do that," he said, "and I might just stick around."

I never wanted a stupid monkey anyway.

2. Hunger Pains

dd this to the things Mama never told me: Sometimes men behave as if they are starving.

When it comes to food, my plate is full and my husband's is licked. At times he reaches panic level, as if famine has struck and emaciation is near.

Last night he came home from work and flung open the cabinet doors. "What are we going to eat for supper?" he cried. "And when are we going to eat? And what about the children – they're probably hungry! Don't we need to go to the store?"

Sometimes it is wise to bite the tongue and ponder in silence. No, WE did not need to go to the store. I needed to go to the store because when he goes with me my cart is filled with crates of crackers, barrels of peanuts, and multiple bunches of bananas and fish … he must have fresh fish, preferably Cobia.

It's possible my husband is suffering from The Gilligan Syndrome, a yet–to–be–identified condition in which food is stashed in case of island stowaway. He probably dreams of being stranded without Ginger and Mary Ann and Mr. and Mrs. Howell and the Skipper and the Professor. He's stuck alone with Gilligan and his crackers and peanuts and bananas and fish, and while he's frantically building a grass hut for his food and hiding it in coconut shells, Gilligan is out chasing minnows.

Back before I ever met my husband, there was another man with whom I spent time. This man was introspective and conflicted and intellectual and kind, but he, too, suffered from irrational hunger.

It was the early eighties, and we were driving back from a movie, *The Jerk*, starring Steve Martin. To me, the humor was superb. Not as funny as King Tut but it was good.I was still laughing halfway home when I noticed the somber look on my boyfriend's face. "Oh, no," I thought to myself. "He's thinking about the time back in fifth grade when he got picked last for kickball, or he can't decide whether to drive out to Lover's Lane or go to the seminary."

"What's wrong now?" I asked, annoyed that Steve Martin was being diminished with each passing minute. "Did your moral compass just blow up or something?"

Silence, followed by a misty tear stuck at the corner of his right eye. Thank God it did not roll down his cheek.

"I'm starving," he said. "I don't think I'm going to be able to make it home. I'm so hungry I feel sick."

I was young and did not know how to process this tidbit of emotional trauma. All I knew was that it made me really, really mad. What about all the times I was hungry? Did I slam on the brakes and screech the tires in the middle of the Interstate, in search of a Whopper exit? Of course not. Instead I'd dig around in the bottom of my purse for a piece of chewing gum or a faded M&M, and that was plenty for me.

I did not understand this phenomenon. Somehow, on a very surface level, I was supposed to feel sorry for my boyfriend because he was hungry. We rode home the rest of the way in silence while I mentally chuckled over Steve Martin's King Tut dance, and then my boyfriend came to his senses and started talking about the glory of the sunset.

My husband is unconflicted and self-sufficient and I can

tolerate his hunger. Still I wish I'd asked Mama this question: *Now that I've captured him, what do I feed him?*

She would have laughed her head off and said, "Go heavy on the fried chicken and mashed potatoes for the first couple of years." And then she would have thrown her head back and laughed again in her famous maniacal laugh, in female recognition of the plight of the hungry man.

3. The Adventures of Love Ape

My husband has turned into Love Ape.

There I was, all snuggled and cozy underneath my soft down comforter when suddenly I was awakened by the primate formerly known as Carl.

"Love Ape lonely," he said, with pouty lip.

"What?" I asked, grabbing my glasses.

"Love Ape lonely," he repeated, and the next thing I knew I was in the clutches of Love Ape's warm embrace.

"Love Ape like," he said with a smile.

I had to admit, this was pretty cute. And besides, it offered potential. Think of the advantages of having a man who would only utter three-word sentences such as "Love Ape lonely," and "Love Ape like." There would be no more political banter, rational discussions about money or decisions about the kids. All I would have to do is keep Love Ape happy and he would be good.

"What would Love Ape like?" I asked. "A banana?"

"No, Love Ape not like banana. Love Ape like you."

"OK, Love Ape. Just shut up and turn out the light and we'll see what we can work out here."

The next morning I was awakened to the wild monkey-like sound of Love Ape's bliss.

"Love Ape happy," he said. "Love Ape love you."

Now tell me, who could resist this? The birth of Love Ape had truly presented a delightful turn in our marriage.

"I love Love Ape," I said, patting him on the head and wondering if this was healthy.

"Love Ape turn out light?" he asked.

"No, Love Ape ... it's morning. The lights won't turn out and I have to make the coffee now."

"Love Ape like coffee," he said.

I was getting a little concerned at this point. Love Ape's sentences had grown into four and five words, and my attraction to the single digit IQ primate was waning. I tucked him back under the covers and slipped out of the bedroom, closing the door behind me.

Ten seconds later he was leaping down the hall, beating his chest and grinning from ear-to-ear. "Love Ape cold! Love Ape need blankie!" he said, grabbing me.

"Look, Love Ape," I said. "You're cute and all, but I like a man who's just a little more civilized from time to time. You know, someone who can discuss politics and help me make decisions about money and the kids."

"Love Ape read newspaper," he said wiping a fake tear from his eye. "You not love Love Ape anymore."

"Oh, come on, Love Ape!" I said, feeling tremendously guilty. "I do love Love Ape – it's just that I need more."

"Love Ape *have* more," he said.

Now I was really concerned. My Love Ape was witty and smart.

"OK, Love Ape, you win. I admit it, I have a man who has it all – curiosity, intelligence, looks, money, and refined primitive skills. I am truly blessed, thank God Almighty. There, are you happy?"

"Love Ape happy," he said triumphantly. "Love Ape real happy."

I wonder, what do monkeys do in the spring?

4. PMS

fter many years of marriage, my husband and I finally laid down a couple of ground rules:

Never have a serious discussion during PMS.

Never have a serious discussion on a Sunday.

Never have a serious discussion, period.

At this point in our lives, we don't have time for serious discussions. We are, however, forced to find creative solutions for PMS.

I have PMS. I only have it one day out of each month, but I make that day count. I'll admit, I kind of like it. The one day out of the month when I can get a way with murder. Well, almost.

PMS is a demon. A lady can feel charming and sweet, and suddenly be overcome by dark, shadowy forces that cause her to behave in an unladylike manner.

She may suddenly utter words she has only read in cheap romance novels.

She may purchase "As Seen on TV" items in mass quantity.

She may even tell her sob story to her son's goldfish.

Go easy on her. It isn't her fault. So what if she sleeps with Hershey Bars? It's only for one day out of the month!

PMS responds well to preventive medicine. Pre-menstrual women like massages, chocolate, cleaning ladies, and nannies. Phrases like, "Let me help you with that, dear," and "Here, put your feet up," and "Is there anything you'd like for me to go out and buy for you?" help immensely.

Doctors will tell you exercise helps, but they're crazy. The best cure for PMS is to crawl into bed and be treated like a queen. The world would be a peaceful place if only men would realize this simple fact.

But men are stubborn. And their stubbornness only intensifies the tender state of PMS. If men would simply give in to all female demands, there would be no more PMS. Until then, consider these helpful pointers when faced with this sensitive yet volatile condition:

You *suspect* you have PMS when...

~ You dream of a chocolate-covered husband.

~ You crave a Hershey Bar while you are eating a Hershey Bar.

~ You drive through the BP station in your pajamas at three in the morning for a Hershey Bar.

You *know* you have PMS when...

~ You flip off your neighbor's yippy dog.

~ You smile when you pour salt on slugs.

~ You grab your teenage son by the shoulders and trumpet like an elephant.

~ PMS affects women differently. Enter my world of hormonal disarray.

Typical PMS scenario number one: It is a normal Monday morning. I am awake, piddling around in the kitchen when suddenly I knock a bowl of Cheerios off the countertop and onto the floor. As if in slow motion, old milk splashes everywhere – onto my hands, my face, my ankles, the cabinets, the sink and the floor. The cats come running and start licking my feet. The feel of sandpaper on my toes at five in the morning is unbearable, and I fall to my knees, pounding the floor.

"Why *me*?" I ask. "Why *me*?"

Typical PMS scenario number two: My husband and I are having a romantic dinner in an expensive restaurant. He's looking into my eyes and making all kinds of promises. And his last paycheck was rather large. Suddenly I remember the time he kept his eyes glued to the Kentucky Derby while I was giving birth fifteen years ago. I grab him by the collar and become livid. "You dog!" I say. "You mangy dog!"

Finally, you know you are in the deep stages of PMS when you rent *Serial Mom* and watch it five times in a row. Perhaps you even know the lines. It's OK.

Grab the remote and a bag of Hershey Bars, crawl into bed, and make the most of it. Just stay away from the scissors.

5. Plasticity

(I) was sitting at my kitchen table with the cat in my lap when the flyer in Monday's paper caught my eye and never let go: *Forty-five Piece Storage and Microwave Set with Measuring Spoons, Cups and Scrapers, all for Only $5.00!* My heart raced, and I and read on: Fifteen-Piece Kitchen Canister Set for Only $3.00! I flung the cat onto the couch and grabbed my car keys.

Some women get a thrill out of clothes. I get a thrill out of cheap plastic.

In record time, I was inside the discount store, forking out my eight bucks for an armload of lightweight bliss. And to think it would last a lifetime! I experienced a Betty Crocker moment, and smiled at my new plastic fortune. Now, I could pack all of our lunches and save bundles of money with which I could purchase bigger and better plastic -- new and improved plastic!

My husband got home at five o'clock and spotted the large box on the table.

"What's that?" he asked.

"It's my new plastic," I confessed. "You are not going to believe the deal I got this time. Eight bucks for sixty pieces of guaranteed lifetime satisfaction! We're all going to start taking our lunch to school and work -- just think of the money we'll save! I thought we'd go out to eat tonight and celebrate."

"Haven't you noticed," he asked, "that we have no more room in this house for plastic or anything else? And do you even begin to grasp that in two days every lid to your new plastic set will be lost or chewed up in the garbage disposal, and that you have no intention of ever making my lunch or anyone else's? Do you realize we eat out every single night, and that since you never cook anymore, you have no leftovers to place inside your plastic toys?"

"I hope your golf balls rot in Hell," I replied.

Unfazed, he stalked over to the refrigerator and stared at all the empty or half-empty plastic dishes. Finally, he picked up a limp carrot from the crisper and took a crunchless bite.

"What's going on here?" he asked, tossing the carrot into the sink. "Why don't you ever cook anymore? And why *do* you buy all that plastic?"

I stared out the window and stuck my chin out, just like my Mama used to do. The chin stance can inflict guilt like no other. "I'm tired of cooking. I work my buns off here in this kitchen, and there's nothing to show for it but a couple of loud burps and fifteen dirty plates. It's just getting old, like me. I don't know why I like plastic. Maybe because it's tough, shiny, and new. Maybe I'm trying to live vicariously through my plastic."

"I'm sorry," he said, kissing me on top of my head. "You're still tough, shiny, and better than new. You've aged well, like a fine wine. And I appreciate what you do -- I just wish you still did it. Maybe I could store fishing lures or golf tees in your plastic fetish. Or we could get a new puppy to chew it all up. Come on, they're getting worried about us at Burger King."

"Fine wine," I thought to myself with a smile. Somehow, he always knows just what to say.

Whoever said vanity was bad never made it to middle age.

6. True Confessions: I Had a Fling with Oxi Clean

I never saw it coming. I was wandering around aimlessly in Wal-Mart when it reached out and grabbed me.

"I can make your life easier," it whispered. "Pick me up. Take me home. Open my lid and I will make you happy."

"It's Oxi Clean!" I screamed.

"Put that down," said my husband, rounding the corner. "What's the matter with you?"

"It's Oxi Clean!" I said. "As seen on TV! I have to have this! Oxi Clean will beautify the carpet, shine the shower, freshen the van, and brighten the deck. It will evaporate stains from clothes. Now I'll be able to get that catsup stain out of your khakis!"

"That's not catsup," he said. "It's blood."

"Oh, really? What happened?"

"I sat down on a toothpick that you left in my seat."

"This is great! Oxi Clean sucks blood out, too!"

By this time, I had my arms wrapped around Oxi Clean and we had become one. It happened that fast. I love the newness of a relationship. The first day, I spot-checked the kitchen floor with Oxi Clean, and marveled at the sparkle of the shine. The second day, I tested a pet stain in the dining room. Amazing! The third day, I washed a load of whites and was almost blinded by the purity of the fabric.

A week passed, and I discovered countless ways to entertain myself with Oxi Clean.

"Why don't you ever clean an *entire* area?" my husband asked. "Like the whole kitchen floor, or *all* the pet stains in the dining room? And don't you think the shower door would look better if you cleaned all of it, rather than just that doughnut-shaped thing in the middle?"

"That's my artwork," I said. "Besides, I prefer spot checks. Entire areas do me in."

Two weeks passed, and we went to the beach on vacation. I found myself yearning for the grainy texture of those little white particles, rubbing against my thumb and index finger. When I got home, I took a bubble bath in Oxi Clean.

My friends noticed a difference. "What's happened to you?" asked Becky. "You seem so dreamy and distracted. And that glow! Are you pregnant or something? Did you inherit a warehouse of Hershey Bars? What *is* it?"

"It's Oxi Clean," I blushed. "You wouldn't believe the light, neutral smell. And the eclectic appeal is unsurpassed."

Two months passed. My husband and I were having dinner in a cozy restaurant, celebrating the mopping of our entire kitchen floor. I had taken the plunge.

"I don't see what's so great about Oxi Clean," he said. "The floor looks great, but Mr. Clean works just as well."

"Are you *crazy?*" I asked. "Mr. Clean is history. I'll never go back to that filmy yellow wimp."

"I'm a little worried about you," he said. "I mean, you never felt this way about Fantastik or Windex."

"Are you *nuts?*" I asked. "Fantastik and Windex have been around for centuries! Oxi Clean is young and new."

"I remember when I felt that way about Bill Dance Bait Spray," he said. "I was convinced the stuff really worked."

"Oh yeah?" I asked. "What changed your mind?"

"I still didn't catch any fish. And the ones I did catch slid off the hook."

"And how long did it take you to figure this out?"

"About three months," he said with a smile. "That's when the new wears off. That's when you realize there's no such thing as new."

Three months passed, and we were once again celebrating at the same cozy restaurant, at the same cozy table.

"It's nice to have you back," my husband said. "That Oxi Clean phase drove me nuts. Tell me, exactly *when* did you realize the thrill was gone?"

"It was when I did that last spot check on the dining room rug. That last pet stain did it for me."

"How so?"

"I finally realized Oxi Clean was just another grainy cleaner that required lots of elbow grease. There, are you happy?"

"Ecstatic," he said. "Nothing beats a little elbow grease and an old-fashioned night crawler."

Ah, the secrets of life.

7. Once Upon a Time

I have always loved "once upon a time" stories. Recently a fellow columnist forwarded me an e-mail that inspired me to write some "once upon a time" stories of my own.

The forwarded e-mail went like this: Once upon a time, a guy asked a girl,"Will you marry me?"

The girl said, "No."

And the guy lived happily ever after and played a lot of golf.

My stories go like this: Once upon a time, a guy asked a girl, "Will you marry me?"

The girl smiled sweetly, batted her Maybelline waterproof eyelashes, and said, "No."

And the girl lived happily ever after and played a lot of golf.

☙ ☙ ☙ ☙ ☙

Once upon a time, a girl asked a guy, "Will you marry me?"

The guy said, "No."

And the girl said, "Good. I just won a $100 dollar bet for asking you."

Once upon a time, a guy asked a girl, "Will you marry me?"

The girl said, "Now why would I want to do that? I spent thirty-years following bread crumbs out of the forest and I finally cut my hair and leaped from the tower without the aid of a man. The Prince who kissed me after my thirty year sleep had maggot breath, and my BMW, which I paid for all by myself, doesn't poof into a pumpkin at midnight. What can you possibly do for me?" she asked.

"I can bake the bread, polish the wood floors, fly to England and buy you the finest antiques, decorate the house, landscape the yard, prepare French cuisine, iron your shirts and arrange your flowers."

And the girl said, "I prefer straight men."

ᬽ ᬽ ᬽ ᬽ ᬽ

Once upon a time, a 75-year-old-man said to a 75-year-old woman, "Will you marry me?"

The 75-year-old woman asked, "Now why would you want to marry me? You're rich, you're distinguished, you're still handsome and you have a hard body. You could have any woman you wanted. Why *me?*"

The 75-year old-man said, "Since I'm in such good physical condition, you'll probably die before I do and I'll still have my money. Your body is not hard and I won't have to worry about swatting other men away. You grew up in the fifties and I'll bet you make a mean cherry pie and wear ironed aprons with no stains. So what do you say – yes or no?"

The woman said, "Yes." A month later, the 75-year-old man died a mysterious death at his kitchen table, where he was found holding a Viagra bottle and eating a piece of lattice-top cherry pie that his 75-year-old wife had baked especially for him. Both of them being devout Baptists, hordes of people attended the funeral and sent flowers and delivered food to the house.

A month later, the 75-year-old widow collected the 2 million insurance policy, flew off to California for an extreme makeover, tossed her apron and her bra into the Pacific and lived happily ever after, high on a cliff overlooking the water.

They say that on a still, cool night, if you listen real carefully, you can hear her singing and smiling to herself, *"Can she bake a cherry pie, Billy Boy, Billy Boy, can she bake a cherry pie, charming Billy? She can bake a cherry pie, quick as a cat can wink an eye, she's a young thing and cannot leave her mother."*

8. Rapunzel Tower

Many of my readers (two, actually) have inquired about my whereabouts. Truth is, I've been in the attic for weeks. It all started when I went up there to do the summer/winter clothes exchange. As luck would have it, my husband came home while the attic door was still open and he conveniently shut it, locking me inside.

It seems I had gotten on his last nerve by speaking in my newly acquired British accent.

Just when I thought I had the cadences and the inflections perfected, he locked me up in my Rapunzel tower.

The defining moment was the morning I was talking incessantly about our two new cats, describing every moment of their waking day to my husband, who is not a morning person. We were sitting on the couch, surrounded by both cats that were ripping up the rug and clawing the furniture and hissing at each other. I got up to pour myself another cup of coffee and my husband tapped me ever so lightly on the buttocks with a wooden spoon. In my perfect British accent, I stood tall and prim and said, "But Father … I have been so good lately!"

There are no words to describe the look he gave me. It was something akin to "I can't handle you anymore but I'm not going to go the traditional route." And so it was that when he came home for lunch on that fateful day, I was performing the winter clothes ritual. Every year it's the same: First I pack up bags of summer clothes from my drawers and consider throwing some of them away. I decide I cannot live without them, although they no longer fit and it's been years since I've worn them, and I pack them away for sentimental value, using a Sharpie to write my name on the white Hefty bags along with the date and the word "summer."

Then I ever so carefully pull down the attic door and climb the annual walk up the stairs. I toss the white summer bags into the attic, and I dig through and find last year's winter clothes in the white Hefty bags along with the date and the word "winter." Then I stop and reflect on what all has happened in the months that have passed and I pray to God that things will get better.

I didn't hear my husband enter the house or turn on the TV. All I heard was the creak of the attic door, closing up and casing me inside. At first I screamed, "Let me out!" but after ten seconds I realized I had a pretty good deal. The lights were on, it wasn't too hot, and there would be no meals to cook or kids to pick up. No phone calls, no e-mail, no inquiries about work, church, or other deadlines.

Actually, it was one of the best times of my life, for in the attic there are old and nostalgic treasures. I read back through the love letters my husband and I wrote to each other while we were engaged, and I laughed hysterically. With great delight I played with my daughters' trolls and braided their hair. I played with the Cabbage Patch Kid, Adena Edna, who bankrupted us back in 1983.

For sustenance, I ate old candy corn and peppermints from the Christmas collection.

It was my complete lack of desperation that freed me from my Rapunzel tower. One day my husband opened the door, pulled down the steps and asked, "Are you ready to come out now?"

In my best British accent I said, "But Father, are you sure?" You seemed so overwhelmed with my very being!"

"I'm sure," he said. "The silence is deafening and the cats are crying for you. Please come down."

And so I made my descent back into the real world where I sit beside my husband every morning and talk his ear off while he stares into space while our new cats tear up our prized possessions.

Not a bad life. Not a bad life at all.

9. Gone Quirky

When my husband married me, he believed I was a normal person. The all-American girl, you might even say. I cooked, cleaned, had houseplants and a job. I went to church, visited my grandparents, donated blood and liked to fish.

He didn't know about my quirks.

He didn't know about the little things that transformed me from the All-American girl into Godzilla.

I thought it best to wait until after the honeymoon to tell him. Here we are, twenty-two years later. The honeymoon may be over but the quirks are bursting with passion.

Here is a partial list of my quirks:

~ Geraldo
~ fat men with toupees
~ fat women with beards
~ generic cola
~ gourmet coffee
~ plastic on lamp shades
~ men with big butts
~ plastic deer in the front yard
~ Channel 2 News
~ spoon clicking
~ ice chomping
~ lip smacking
~ gum popping

~ doctors who make you take off your shirt to check a sinus infection

~ people who weigh 400 pounds, yet crusade against ingredients in soap and shampoo

~ e-mail prayer-threat-chain letters

~ mispronunciation of "nuclear"

~ Tide commercials

~ acrylic sweaters

~ bald-headed babies with bows stuck on their heads

My quirks are manifested in the following scenarios:

My husband and I are lying in bed, watching the news. I am almost asleep when suddenly Geraldo's sneering little face appears on TV. As usual, he's making it all up as he goes along, smiling because he's getting away with it. I can see straight through this conniving creep with the curled-out moustache.

"Shut up, Geraldo!" I yell. "You don't have me fooled, you slimy cheap trick. Just shut up!"

"Calm down," my husband says. "He'll go off in a minute. You know they never keep him on for long."

Scenario number two could go something like this:

It's allergy season again and I've been sitting in the doctor's office for two hours. I've examined the ceiling, played with the Popsicle sticks, stolen a handful of Kleenex and read *Children's Bible Stories*. At long last, in walks "Dr. Bob" with a confident grin on his face. "What seems to be the problem?" he asks, toying with his stethoscope.

"I can't breathe," I say. "My head is all stopped up and my eyes are watery."

"Ah," he says with a broad smile. "You've come to the right place. Just take off your shirt and your sinuses will be clear in

JULIA LEE

no time at all."

"Last time I looked, doc, my nose was on my face."

Sometimes my quirks exasperate my husband. "Is there anything that doesn't annoy you?" he asks.

"Of course there are things that don't annoy me," I say. "I like penguins, Johnny Depp, zinnias and sunflower seeds."

You can guess which three items I got for Mother's Day.

It's OK to be quirky. At least my quirks are entertaining. I mean, how far can you go with a tube of toothpaste that gets squeezed in the middle?

I'll take Geraldo any day.

10. Competition

In many cities across America, there are men who play with dolls. Somehow, this makes me feel better about myself. Knowing that there are men who play with dolls reminds me that my own quirky behavior is within reason, and therefore correctible.

There are many things I wish to correct about myself, and a good starting point would be stupid competitive behavior, particularly in the realm of marriage. While most people compete in sports and in business, my competitive areas are limited to food, parking spaces, and determining who is more fatigued at the end of the day – my husband or I.

Under ideal circumstances, when both my husband and I are somewhat rested and cognizant of The Golden Rule, there are no problems in the area of competitive fatigue. But under normal circumstance, when we are both exhausted and The Golden Rule is a blur on the mental horizon, things get hairy.

The mental fatigue competitive issue reached epidemic proportions a couple of days ago. He was tired and I was tired, and rather than listen compassionately to my tale of woe, he sat glued to the TV, clinching the remote in his hand, which led me to make a killer comment. "I got killed yesterday and my funeral's Thursday," I said.

"I got killed last week and my funeral was Monday," he replied. Then he added, "And if you play 'Moon River' one more time I'm going to poke your eyeballs out."

"Well, heavenly days!" I said. "We have an emotional disconnect in our marriage!"

"It'll be OK," he said. "It always is. I'll scratch your back for five hours and you'll forget all about it until this time next month."

And the thing is, I know he's right. One of the advantages of being married for twenty three years is perspective: After time, you know what is important and what is not, and you come to recognize no-win situations. I sense that I have recently made great strides in the area of competitive fatigue behavior, and it is my personal goal to tackle competitive food behavior next. This one is going to be much tougher for me.

I never was one of those girls who went out on dates, afraid to eat too much. I never picked at my food or chewed delicately while smiling flirtatiously at my date. Oh, I used a fork and I put the napkin in my lap, but I also cleaned my plate, often before my date did. I remember one date in particular, where the guy had driven me to a nearby town, only to whip into the Shoney's parking lot. I bit my tongue because I was hungry, and after our order arrived I began to wolf down my food while he sat and stared at me.

"What are you looking at?" I asked between bites of jumbo shrimp and onion rings.

"It embarrasses me to eat in front of other people," he said shyly.

"No problem," I said. "I'll just eat your food, too."

Surprisingly, the man asked me out again but I refused. I'd always known how to handle a hungry man, and there was a certain turn-off in encountering a non-hungry man. I was in lost territory that did not even intrigue me enough to explore the terrain.

My husband is always hungry, and I like that. The problem is he eats fast, which kicks my competitive food behavior into gear, and I find myself trying to out-eat him, my eyes glued to the biggest piece of chicken or that last helping of mashed potatoes, which is MINE.

My competitive food issue will take time, perhaps even a lifetime. It may even prevent me from dealing with my competitive parking lot behavior.

But it'll be OK, because it always is. And in many cities across America, there are men who play with dolls.

11. Sweetness

I t's January and there's not much to do besides sleep and go out to eat and eavesdrop on the conversations of people around you. The other day I was in a coffeehouse waiting for my gingerbread latte with whipped cream, pretending to read the newspaper. I was actually listening to the conversation between the two young women behind the counter who were talking about their boyfriends, of all things.

The dreamy blonde said to the sensible brunette, "I loved it when my boyfriend called me 'Sweetness' this morning. I was like, 'Oooh, yeah!'" She gushed about being called "Sweetness" for two or three minutes while the brunette piled my latte high with whipped cream and sprinkled nutmeg on top. It was obvious that while she was happy for her co-worker, she yearned to be called "Sweetness," also.

Simply put, there was no turning back for the blonde. The sound of the word "Sweetness," whispered softly into her ear at just the right moment, was brilliant and had her seriously hooked. She will re-live the moment over and over, possibly for the rest of her life. Gentlemen, take note.

A woman remembers the first time a man whispers, "I love you" into her ear. We remember the first time a man calls us "Baby" or "Sweetness," and we begin to cook elaborate French cuisine for that man. Pounds suddenly melt off of our bodies because we are "just not hungry." We are desperately and hopelessly in love and very blind in this early stage, but that's part of the plan.

If the "twenty-years-down-the-road stage" had been placed at the beginning of the relationship, none of us would have ever been conceived. It is the same principle that keeps us from murdering our teenage children after having bonded with them as newborn babies and cuddly toddlers.

The order of life is no accident, in most cases. There are exceptions, such as the 67-year-old woman who recently gave birth. I'd bet money her husband isn't smiling and whispering "Sweetness" into her ear, while she whips up a Galette des Rois (King's Cake) in the kitchen.

Chances are, that old mama's probably sacked out on the couch, trying to remember if she really had a baby, and if so, where is it? Good grief. If I had a baby at this stage of the game, I'd have to name it "What's his name."

Everything changes but some things remain the same. One of my favorite songs is "The River" by Bruce Springsteen, in which he sings about his younger days of taking Mary "down to the river" for a moonlight swim. It is a metaphor of days gone by, and one to which we hopefully can all relate, for those who never experienced a moonlight swim missed out on an experience that is akin to being called "Sweetness" in the wee morning hours.

It's never too late go for the moonlight swim at any age, and I might just grab my husband and take the plunge when the weather gets warm.

But it's January, so here's a toast to youth, that blind and delicious stage of early love, "Sweetness," and moonlight swims.

12. Waxing Gibbous

Thanks to an e-mail that I recently received, my life now makes perfect sense. Specifically, the e-mail linked me to a website called "On the Day You Were Born," or in other words, "The Ultimate Case of Too Much Information."

I now know that at the moment of my conception, which occurred on or about November 5, that my parents were either listening to "The Purple People Eater" by Sheb Wooley, or "Don't" by Elvis Presley.

Thanks to "On the Day You Were Born," I know every single detail about my life thus far. I know how old I am in dog years, how many BTUs the candles on my next birthday cake will produce and the number of hours, minutes and seconds I have lived.

I have learned about my life path compatibility and that my life path number is 5. I am least compatible with those whose life path numbers are 2, 4, 6, 11 and 22. In other words, my husband and children, every single one of them. Furthermore, I have learned that my husband's life path number is compatible with all of our children's life path numbers, and that is why they have always ganged up against me.

After studying the "On the Day You Were Born" stats for my husband and children, I became convinced that my parents were indeed listening to "Don't" by Elvis Presley at the moment of my conception. Now I understand the source of the original opposition and resistance that has tainted my life.

There is nothing I can do. My *life path* number is 5, and that's that. The good news is, I now have proof that my husband is, well, stubborn. Here is what his life path number says about him: You have the kind of will power that is often mistaken for sheer stubbornness.

On the day my husband was born, the moon's phase was full, and on the day I was born the moon was waxing gibbous. I don't know what that means but it sounds gooey to me. I would have preferred a new moon or a crescent moon, but waxing gibbous is what I got. At the moment of my conception, somewhere near the end of "Don't" by Elvis Presley, my mother probably looked out the window and said, "Gad, the moon is waxing gibbous."

"Gad" was my mother's favorite word, and she said it whenever she became alarmed, which was approximately every three seconds. My sisters and I always wondered what "gad" meant. My mother also used other words and expressions too numerous to mention, but one of them was "ookie doo," which somehow reminds me of "waxing gibbous."

Some information is best left unknown, such as the details of the moment of our conception. The past is the past and all we can do is march forward with our incompatible life numbers. Still, I can't help but wonder how it might have been if the moon had been full and my parents had been listening to "Volare" by Domenico Modugno.

I'll never know, and that's a very good thing.

13. Big Ass Feet

Recently I read two articles on men and women, both written by women, of course. One article was about how to get closer to a man in five minutes or less, and the other was about how to break up with a man and remain friends. In short, womanhood defined: Come here, come here, come here; get away, get away, get away!

But alas! This is our greatest form of entertainment. It is what we do. Some men call it manipulation. Some call it cold and cruel. I call it estrogen. But lately my estrogen supply seems to be diminishing and I am becoming more and more practical.

I am weary of stupid, cutesy ideas and suggestions. The gap between men and women could be bridged if only we would simplify our thinking.

The article on how to get closer in five minutes included suggestions such as timed kissing, fighting with feather pillows, flipping through your wedding album to look at old snapshots, and popping the song that was played at your wedding into your CD player.

All I can say is whoever wrote this is an idiot. First of all, if my husband and I had an actual pillow fight, we would never get to the timed kissing part because we would be dead. Second of all, if we looked at our wedding photo we would be reminded of how young and innocent and attractive we once were, and we would become depressed and go eat Mexican food. And third of all, the song that was played at our wedding, at my mother's insistence, was "The Hallelujah Chorus."

In truth, the best way to get closer to your man is to pounce on top of him and belt out the Enjoli song: "I can bring home the bacon, fry it up in a pan, and never let him forget he's a man, 'cause I'm a woman." If you are too young to know about the Enjoli song, you don't need to be reading this column.

Moving on to my favorite article on how to break up and still remain friends, I am struck by the initial question: But why do I wish to remain friends? Is it not my mission to depart from this man?

Suggestions included occasionally staying in touch, preferably by phone, and writing down rational reasons to break up, stated only in positive terms.

This, too, is stupid. We are trying to break up, so let's get to the point! I have found the following tactics to be not only immensely helpful, but genuinely foolproof:

Take his chin in your hand and tilt it ever so gently so that he is gazing into your eyes. An inevitable somber moment that is full of wonder and intrigue will occur, and it is at this point that you should say to him, "I have no idea if I'm a man or a woman, and frankly, neither does my gynecologist."

My second favorite method of getting a man to back off is to take him shopping with you to a ritzy mall. Insist that he accompany you along the way, then plop yourself down in a chair in the shoe department at the finest store in the mall. It is then that you will blow a giant pink bubble with your Bazooka wad and say to the male shoe salesman, "Got any shoes for my big-ass feet?" Works every time.

Guaranteed or your man back.

P(A)RT ii
Family: The Cold Hard Truth

1. Frozen Nipples

There are so many things I wish I'd known before it was too late. But before I could utter the words, "Not tonight, honey – my entire body is packed in Peruvian mud," I had significantly populated the earth.

Today's women have so much more information than I did – there are tons of books and articles all over the place. All I had was *Parents* magazine, which I did subscribe to but never read because I thought it was stupid and it made me feel guilty because as a mother, I did things in a different way.

I never wanted to be one of those mothers who strolled their babies to the park and sat on a bench with other mothers while whining about our sore nipples. Who wants to hear about such things? Although I have given birth on many occasions, I do not bask in the glory of the moment and bore others with the details, as some women do.

These are women who for whatever reason think other people actually give a rip about their botched epidural or upside-down-baby or their sore nipples. News flash: People don't care. Your mother may possibly care, but no one else does, so shut up.

I recently ran across this breast-feeding tip from a new mother: "A hot shower will help the milk flow, but if your breasts are sore after nursing, place a bag of frozen peas across your chest."

I wonder, would that be purple hull or plain old English peas? I can just picture my husband back in the early days, coming home from work seeing me sacked out in a chair with a bag of frozen peas across my chest.

No doubt he would have said, "Hot little mama, that's so sexy I'm going to call a babysitter right now and arrange for us to go away for the weekend so that we can have another baby and look forward to more frozen vegetables atop your aching breasts! The vision of frozen okra pods is simply driving me wild – where do you want to stay, the Mariott or the Sheraton?"

Here's another tip I read from one of the mothers of today: "Women who seek help have a higher success rate." Well, duh! Has the world simply gotten so old that we have run out of stuff to write about? This type of advice drives me nuts, in the same way women sitting on park benches and whining about their sore nipples drives me nuts.

And all I've got to say to the woman who puts frozen peas on her breasts is that she ain't seen nothin' yet and she might as well jump into the freezer and stay there until her baby has cycled completely through the teenage years.

Sore nipples don't hold a candle to teenage insurance rates and vampire wannabees and sagging britches and rap music. Better enjoy "Rock-a-Bye Baby" while you can, because it gets nasty. It gets so nasty you'd give your left nipple for the Humpty Dumpty days.

So go ahead and sit back until your frozen peas thaw out on your chest. Just remember to cook 'em real slow after you wake up, and around five o'clock that night stick a skillet of cornbread in the oven to go with them. Slice up a tomato and a cucumber and a tad of onion, for onion is not sexy, and your husband will love the Southern comfort.

In fact, he'll love it so much that in no time you'll find

yourself spending hours in the frozen section, just looking for that perfect vegetable to soothe your aching nipples that your latest newborn has inflicted upon you.

2. Life Its Own Self

My son has turned into Socrates.

This morning at breakfast he stood up from eating his Frosted Flakes, made one final chomp and said, "Every day should be called tomorrow, except for yesterday and today."

My other son was standing by the sink making gargling noises for no logical reason, and my teenage daughter was flinging stuff around in the bathroom. "Where's the hairdryer?" she yelled. "Have you seen my contact case? And where is my toothbrush? Have you been using my toothbrush again? Mom! Come here!"

I try to appease this child but it never works. She's picky – the type who buys Clinique without the bonus. Lately she spends most of her spare time hugging her boyfriend in the middle of the street, like a parting scene from a war movie.

I meet her in the bathroom and say in a low voice, "I think your toothbrush is under the sink, beside the Listerine. Be quiet, or you'll wake your father."

"Would you stop talking about mouthwash like it's a covert operation?" she says. "And what's wrong with waking up Dad? He should have to get up like the rest of us."

"Shhhh!" I say. "I'm listening to Dan Fogelberg and Carole King, and he'll want to turn on the stock market channel."

"You're goofy, Mom. Think outside the box."

What box?

Mornings are chaotic. My mother-in-law tells me she misses

the hustle and bustle, and even in the midst of my chaos I can understand why. Maybe I'm lucky to realize it never gets any better or easier. It just gets quieter.

The kids leave for school and my husband wakes up and lodges himself at the computer. I have a vision of him in thirty years, sitting gray-headed at the computer and grumbling, "Takes fifteen minutes to turn her on and I still can't remember which button to push."

Am I getting old or what? Am I goofy or premenopausal or is this just the way things are? Why doesn't anyone tell us the truth about midlife? Why didn't anyone tell us we'd still be squeezing zits at forty? Why didn't they tell us about the middle-age flatulence that would pollute our lives?

Probably because they were too busy. In the midst of the chaos of teenagers and hormones and jobs and homework, they didn't find the time.

I feel compelled to write it all down and take lots of pictures, because I tend to forget the day-to-day details, and I want proof.

If we knew about the gray hair and the gas, we might not marry. And if we never married, we wouldn't have children. Duh. It's that survival of the species thing again.

I used to yearn for perfection. I wanted the perfect husband, the perfect children, the perfect body, the perfect casserole. Yet in my quest for the masterpiece, I found disappointment. There was always that longing, and then I realized it was only a longing. Perfection is rare, like a great family picture, or a pile of red and golden leaves on a cool November day in the heart of middle Tennessee.

Some things are best figured out by ourselves.

3. Order of Birth

Motherhood is hell. No matter how hard I try, I can't be everywhere at once and I am ridden with guilt. And my second born doesn't help matters any.

"You know nothing about me," she says in a "woe is me" moment. "You have no idea what my life is about."

"Gee, you're right," I say. "Sixteen years ago I looked up from my banana split and said, "Wow! There's a new baby on my couch. Where on earth did it come from?"

It's no wonder so many men run away. Women would run, too, but they'd die of guilt.

There's something to these birth order theories.

When that firstborn explodes onto the scene, worlds are rocked and that little baby is smart enough to recognize this immediately. Yes, even a seven-pound infant can see that her parents are babbling idiots and quickly take advantage of the situation.

Until the second born comes along, the world is served to the firstborn on a silver platter. It's quite possible the child will spend a lifetime looking for that silver platter after it disappears, and it will disappear.

It will disappear because the parents will one day get tired and run out of money. And when they finally do get enough money to bring back the silver platter, they realize it was a bad idea to begin with.

The good thing about the second child is that it is possible to recognize mistakes from the firstborn experience.

The second-born child is different from the first. She, too, immediately sizes up the situation for opportunity, but doesn't see the vastness the first child saw. There is only a glimpse of a silver platter, and therefore it doesn't come to mean as much to this child.

The second child benefits from the guilt the mother feels upon giving birth the second time around. It isn't the same as the first time. Most women won't admit this, but they secretly feel something is wrong because it isn't the same. Oh, they love the baby and all, but they make the mistake of comparing it to that magical firstborn moment.

I used to feel guilty about this until I realized my magical firstborn moment was actually a Percodan high. Consequently, I decided to request a Percodan two hours after giving birth to each of my children, right about when the epidural wore off. I have never regretted this decision.

Still, I felt somewhat guilty after giving birth the second time. Was I doing this right? Did I love the second baby as much as the first one? Did I give the first child the attention she needed? Was Heinz baby food really as good as Gerber? Pampers or Luvs? The list was endless and the second child seized the opportunity.

This is why, sixteen years later, she says cruel things like, "You have no idea what my life is about."

Children seize their mothers' deepest fears and ride them as far as they can, enjoying every minute of it. I tend to forget this fact and react on a rather emotional level.

"How could you say such a thing?" I ask. "I've spent a lifetime watching you grow, and I know everything about you. After all I've done for you! Doesn't back labor mean *anything* to you?" Enter the third child.

The third child never sees an opportunity or a silver platter, because her parents are wise and near bankruptcy. This is why the third child is innovative and keen.

Everyone should have a third child, because they are a joy to raise. They learn much from the mistakes of the two older siblings and use it to their full advantage. Third children are appreciative, affectionate, generous, undemanding, and near perfect.

I am a third child, so I should know.

4. Topless Corn

L ate July, 1971. With the exception of cousin Lon, the womenfolk are headed to the back forty to pick corn.

My aunt is driving the tractor with Lon by her side. The rest of us are on the trailer. The pond has flooded, and it is the brownest water I have ever seen. Is it because the pond is small, and large cows that are not potty-trained stand in it frequently to cool off?

My mother says, "Well, good night, what are we gonna do? We can't get around the pond! We'll have to walk, and I am about to burn up! I do not believe I can stand this! Gad!"

"Oh no," laughs the aunt in a haughty voice. She is feeling some serious girl power behind the wheel of the tractor. "You just hold on there, old gal. We'll make it."

With Lon's assistance, she cuts around the pond like a pro. My grandfather respects her work ethic and expertise, and places her ability level on a much higher pedestal than the men in the family.

"Well Lord, Hon," says our great-aunt Tut. "Do you reckon we can stand the heat?"

Granny giggles. My girl cousin and I roll our eyes.

"I do believe this is the hottest day of my life!" My mother says. "I am about to burn up!"

The tractor pulls us down the lane, and it is a bumpy but pleasant stretch. Lon jumps off to unlock the gate, and we're off again. We come to pond number two, but this one is surrounded by trees. The back forty is over to the right. We're almost there, and we start gathering up our buckets. The beans are coming in, and the okra is ready. But the big news is the corn: Corn is sacred. They don't even let me pick it because of the damage I might inflict. Fine with me.

Cuz and I pluck off a couple of green beans, and walk around, observing. Great-aunt Tut is plowing through the beans like a beaver in a teakwood forest. "Lord, these beans are nice! Look at this one, Hon!" she cries, holding it up to the light.

Over in the cornfield, my mother says, "I cannot stand this anymore – I am having a hot flash! I'm telling you, I am about to burn up!" She rips off her shirt and throws it at the ground. "Whew!" she says. "That's a little better."

Granny snickers, "That child's been going through the change for ten years. Gotten more mileage out of it than anyone I ever knew."

I wonder what I possibly have to look forward to in life.

The aunt succumbs to the heat and sails her shirt into the wind. Playtex Cross-Your- Hearts come in many shapes and sizes, but they stop at EEE, so Granny and Aunt Tut remain fully clothed.

Finally we finish, and my mother and aunt put their shirts back on. "I am *wet with sweat*," my mother says. "Look here!"

My mother does not look wetter than anyone else. We ride back to the house, the aunt driving and singing "Catfish Floatin' Down the River," and Lon steering the wheel of the tractor. He is three years old.

"Lord, Hon, do you reckon we can fix all these beans?" asks Aunt Tut.

"Why sure we can, Sister. We always do," says Granny.

We get back to the house, drink plenty of ice water, and sit out under the maple tree, snapping beans. It is one of the best moments of my life, definitely in the top ten.

"I think I'm finally starting to cool off," my mother says.

"I'm sure you are, Hon," says Granny. "I'm sure you are."

5. Big Purple Box

People talk about family values and profanity and nudity on TV, but it's the commercials we need to be wary of. In fact, the sanitary pad people should stop making commercials and have their own weekly sitcom.

Take sanitary pads for example. Oh, sure, no one wants to think or talk about sanitary pads – the very words conjure up yuck. But still, the time has come to address the subject that no one wants to talk about but is forced to watch on TV.

Back when I was a kid, there was only one sanitary pad, or napkin as they were called, and they came in a big purple box that sat in the bathroom behind the clothes hamper. I never knew what was in the big purple box – I just assumed it was part of the bathroom because it was always there and it never changed. Just a large purple box that somehow seemed to say in a loud voice, "I am here."

Whenever I'd ask Mama what was in the big purple box, she'd tell me to go watch *Romper Room,* and I did, because I was more intrigued by Miss Nancy and her magic mirror than the contents of the purple box. Even today, the notion of Miss Nancy waving at me and saying my name intrigues me more than the purple box.

Somewhere along the way, though, people started talking about the purple box, and the whole can of worms busted wide open. Suddenly there were blue boxes and white boxes and all different kinds of brand names. Somehow, sanitary napkins had babies called panty-liners, and eventually they sprouted wings.

Today's sanitary napkins are high-tech indeed. Not only do you have to stand there and ponder in the aisle for two hours over which brand or what style to buy, you have to be able to speak Spanish to decide.

But folks, things have gone too far. It is time to return to the simplicity of the big purple box. Just the other day, a Sunday in fact, my son and I were sitting side-by-side on the couch when a sanitary pad commercial came on. This in itself did not embarrass either of us, for we are now desensitized to the world of the sanitary pad.

But this sanitary pad accomplished the impossible. No, it did not have babies and no, it did not sprout wings. It morphed into a recliner that gave the illusion of peace, love, happiness and contentment. Seriously. I was watching TV with my son and I saw a sanitary pad evolve into a recliner. I was so astounded that I said, "Anybody who believes that crap is crazy."

But some things never change. Even in today's world of panty-liners with baby wings Espanola, and even with pads that turn into recliners, I still find myself at the grocery store, tucking the box away discreetly beneath the frozen pizza.

It's best that way.

6. Do Be a Do Bee

Never give up.

— Winston Churchill and 5 zillion other people

As a child, I spent countless hours in front of the old black and white TV in the living room, watching Miss Nancy on *Romper Room*. Those were some of the best days of my life – my two older sisters were in school, and I was home alone with my mother, where I had her all to myself.

Although Miss Nancy was my idol, I found it hard to emulate her. Early on, I struggled with being a "Do Bee." Still, she taught me it was a worthy aspiration, and to this day I try to be a "Do Bee."

My favorite part of *Romper Room* was the end. Every day, Miss Nancy would get out her magic mirror and wave to all the good little boys and girls out there in Do Bee Land. At this point, I would sit up and lean toward the TV, watching and waiting and hoping and praying that just once, she would call out my name. In my heart of hearts, I just knew that she would, yet it never happened.

I never gave up hope, but as time went by, I got mad. "Why wasn't I a good Do Bee?" I would ask myself. "What's so great about Billy and Tommy and Becky and Sue?"

One day, in desperation, I spotted my sisters' dollar bills on the white vinyl chair in the living room. My mother had actually paid them for helping her vacuum. *Romper Room* had gone off, and my mother was outside pinching her petunias. Quickly, I turned on the vacuum cleaner and sucked those dollar bills right up, with great satisfaction.

If I couldn't make Do Bee status, then I was going to have a hell of a time being a Don't Bee. Now I'm not saying it was Miss Nancy's fault that I became a Don't Bee. Lord knows, there's no telling what kind of evil acts I would have committed if she had not introduced me to the Do Bee concept. I just wanted to hear her call out my name. Just once, and then I would be happy.

I got older, and had to go to school and leave the comfort of Mama and Miss Nancy. At school, I would dream of the days when I would be stretched out on the floor in my pajamas with feet, stuffing crackers or Frosted Flakes into my mouth and praying that Miss Nancy would call out my name.

With great trepidation, I finally grew up and gave up the notion of the magic mirror. Magic was for children and for dreamers, I sensibly told myself. But deep inside, I still believed that one day, Miss Nancy would call out my name.

Currently, the Do Bee struggle continues, but I no longer see myself as a Don't Bee. Goodness is an aspiration, a goal we may never fully reach. Miss Nancy taught me that.

Two weeks ago, I was stuffing Ritz crackers into my mouth while nonchalantly checking my e-mail. Lo and behold, there was a message from **THE** Miss Nancy! Turns out, she has a relative here in Maury County who had sent her a column of mine that made reference to Miss Nancy and the *Romper Room* years.

In a matter of seconds, I went temporarily insane and became a five-year-old again. At first, I just stared at the e-mail with my mouth open, completely astonished. Then, I hit the reply button and asked, "Miss Nancy, is that really *you*? After all these years, are you finally calling out my name?"

She e-mailed me back and assured me that yes, it really was her. She also thanked **ME** for remembering the *Romper Room* years.

I have regained my sanity and I am living in the midst of a very good dream. Miss Nancy has called out my name, and I am a happy, happy girl.

7. It's Only A glass

here is compensation in life, and age brings us wisdom along with age spots and varicose veins. With luck, we learn to open our eyes and take a close and honest look at our lives to determine if we need to reprioritize.

I get attached to inanimate objects – often cheap, inanimate objects, and a few years ago I bought some precious cherry glasses at Big Lots. The glasses reminded me of the jelly glasses of my childhood – the ones my grandmother kept in her pantry alongside the cherry pitcher that she never actually used. It was just a permanent fixture in her house that somehow symbolized familiarity, peace, stability and love.

But I was never around when my grandparents were young, with small children of their own. My view of them was idyllic, because I knew them when they were at that stage of life where reprioritization had taken place, and they had simplified and gotten rid of baggage. Everyone should be so lucky to be influenced by people like this.

I bought six cherry glasses at Big Lots and I now have one, sitting high and lone in a cabinet beside an antique nut grinder. At first it bothered me to hear the shattering of glass on the basement floor, followed by the stampede up the stairs. "Do you know where the broom is?" my youngest would ask. "I broke a cherry glass."

Together we would search for the broom and sweep up every shard of glass, and I would remind him to only take plastic glasses to the basement. "I'm sorry Mom," he'd say. "I know how much you like those cherry glasses."

"It's OK," I'd say. "Just don't take any more of them to the basement." But old habits die hard for children and adults, and my youngest would grab a cherry glass and race downstairs with no thought of plastic.

I'm one of the lucky ones. By the time he broke the fifth glass, I realized it didn't matter and that after all the glasses were broken, the love of my grandparents would live intact in my heart forever.

It was nighttime when the fifth glass fell, and this time my son trudged up the stairs, unable to look at me. "Have you seen the broom?" he asked in self-deprecation. "I broke another cherry glass."

"It's only a glass," I said. "Don't worry about it – we'll clean it up and I'll put the last one way up high, where it won't be easy to reach. And if you ever break that one, that'll be OK, too."

He was relieved to know I wasn't disappointed, and once again I thought of my grandparents, but this time in a different light. I knew them when they had drawn certain conclusions, but I was not privy to the experiences that had led to those conclusions. Perhaps at one time they cared too much about the cherry glasses, and were lucky enough to learn the value of loving a small child before it was too late.

I have a hard time with goodbyes, and I surround myself with cheap inanimate objects that remind me of the love that was once there. It's all very tacky – a green plastic rhinoceros that I got at age two adorns the TV in our bedroom. And it was only recently that I fully realized my bedposts were decorated with hats belonging to my grandfather and my husband.

I was sick in bed a few weeks ago, forced to lie still for a few hours, and when I looked at the green rhinoceros and the hats I started to cry. "What's wrong?" my husband asked.

"I don't know," I said. "That rhinoceros is the ugliest thing in the world, and you've never cared if I kept it on top of the TV. And the hats – I just noticed the hats hanging on the bedpost. Somehow I look at the hat and see the person who wore them so clearly, and somehow that makes me cry."

"You're a sentimental girl," he said, "and that's OK."

For the glass will break and the hat will hang empty, but the love will live on forever.

8. Neptune

I have a child that I did not actually give birth to. One day in 1987 I was standing out in my back yard when a baby fell from the planet Neptune fell and landed into my arms.

He has fit in well with the rest of the family, and strangely, he looks just like my husband. I love this kid and all, but he and I are polar opposites and I can never predict what he going to say or do.

He is quiet and healthy and many people do not even know about this one. Oh, they know about the some of the others all right – the ones who have run over people's feet with their cars and that sort of thing, but they do not know about Neptune because the squeaky wheel gets the grease and Neptune rarely squeaks.

I basically just have to feed him and buy him a new pair of pants every week because he keeps growing and growing and growing and growing. I love to gaze up at him and wonder if his head will one day reach all the way up into the clouds, back toward Neptune.

Sometimes he is stubborn and discipline is a challenge. I pull a kitchen chair up in front of him, stand up tall and get in his face. "If you don't go do your homework right now," I say, "I am going to pinch your nose." He gives me that "You're pathetic" look and slinks away to do his homework. He's that simple.

To say that he has a dry sense of humor is not enough. The other day we were driving down the road and I was secretly thrilled by the way his knees were wedged into the glove compartment, even though his seat was scooted all the way back. I said, "There's something I never told you. When you were little I put Miracle Grow in your bottle."

"That explains it," he said, with a hint of a dreamy smile.

This kid deserves a column devoted solely to him because he has been quiet and good and undemanding, and I've always felt guilty about the bird thing.

When Neptune's baby brother was two years old, we were having an idyllic winter moment, stretched out on the floor in front of the fire, coloring.

To my horror, I looked to my right and there beside me was a Parakeet head. I then did what any good mother would do – I picked up the head and flung it into the fire behind me and went right on coloring. Baby Brother never said a word and neither did Neptune, because they had no idea I had cremated the bird. In twenty minutes or so, Neptune looked up at his empty birdcage and asked, "Where's my bird?"

"It's in the pire," said Baby Brother, who also went right on coloring.

"What's it doing in the fire?" he screamed.

"Mama threw it in there," said Baby Brother.

I could not believe this kid had watched me throw a bird head into the fire without saying a word, then at the age of two would use it as evidence.

"There was nothing I could do," I said. "The cats got hold of another one but this time they left the head. I was only trying to spare you the pain."

When Neptune was little he spent the night with my sister. The next morning she took him to the bakery and asked, "Do you want a doughnut?"

"What's a doughnut?"

"You know what a doughnut is, Neptune! It's one of those round things with a hole in the middle. Surely your mother feeds them to you."

"Oh, yeah! I'll take ten of them."

When Neptune was in first grade he got a U in spelling.

"What does "U' mean?" he asked.

"It means U did real good," I said. "I'm so proud of you that I think we should celebrate by going to get a hot fudge sundae from Baskin Robbins."

Neptune is spatially gifted. At age five he built a six- foot motorized Ferris wheel from K-nex that graced the middle of the den for two months. Religious zealots would come to our door and I'd whisper, "No you can't come in right now -- we've got our carnival running in there.'

Neptune is now a quite average boy. Recently his older sister said to me, "You know, it's funny. I think Neptune is actually going to be the most normal one of us all."

Things change, but this week I would agree.

9. Biscuits

Life is hard for us all. Still, it might have been easier if my mother had warned me of certain truths, to save me from being blindsided by inevitabilities along the way. She could have told me that while fathers are watching football games, mothers will cry over their children until the end of time.

Surely she knew that in order to make good biscuits, you have to make them at least once a week. Biscuits know when they haven't been made lately.

How easy it would have been for her to tell me that marriage is like Kansas; a tornadic zone in which I would need to prepare myself: get better warning systems, build stronger storm shelters, and put my head under the pillow when it all starts to fly.

And of all things, why didn't she tell me about hot flashes? She never told me there would come at time when I would awaken at two in the morning in a grimy sweat with a cat stuck to my head on one side and my husband stuck to my back on the other. How was I to know that I would one day dream of an icy lake that I could plunge into, or yearn to roll naked through the snow?

She should have warned me about putting things on the back burner, things such as politics, religion, sex, and any kind of conflict whatsoever. She should have told me that the back burner can only hold so much, and that it might one day blow a fuse and nearly burn the house down if I didn't rearrange things.

It would have been nice to know, early on, that loyalty is a rare thing indeed, and that I would be lucky to have at least one loyal friend and three loyal acquaintances. But my mother did not tell me these things, and I have discovered them on my own. Like many women, I have had to learn to be my own mother, and so far it appears to be working.

They say experience is the best teacher and Lord knows I've had plenty of that. I'm just happy to be here, alive and well and able to pass on certain truths and inevitabilities to my children and any other conceivable beneficiaries.

So in addition to the truth about football, biscuits, hot flashes and back burners, I tell my children to listen to themselves, and to never completely turn down the volume of that little voice inside their heads that tells them who they are and what to do, for it is that voice alone that will carry them through the tornadic zones and rearrange the back burners of their lives.

I have been lucky in life, in spite of the lack of my mother's advice. A wise woman once said to me, "I want your voice to get louder," and it did. For there was a time in my life when the volume button was turned off, and I listened to anyone and everyone but myself.

Turning that button back on and turning up the volume was the best thing I ever did in my life, although the music was not pleasant to everyone's ears. It would have been nice if my mother had told me she wanted my voice to get louder, but she never did and she never will.

Perhaps she never learned that lesson herself.

10. Dysfunction Junction

I'm proud of my dysfunctional family. Without them, I wouldn't be who I am today. Seriously.

We had lots of the usual stuff – marital discord, various and sundry addictions, and one twisted poodle, whose bedroom was bigger than mine. She ate T-bones for breakfast while I was lucky to get a couple of toast crumbs. She wore a red wool coat in the winter and sunglasses in the summer. Tinkerbell was her name, and my mother adored her. Dogs, it seemed, were easier than children. They didn't talk back, they didn't have crying jags or slumber parties, and they growled at strangers.

Tinkerbell was the wheelbase in our family, and the rest of us were spokes. This was by design. Much easier to focus on a dog than to look inward. No, the only thing our family ever looked deep inside of was the refrigerator. Mama was a great Southern cook and food was a comfort.

I've spent years coming to terms with my dysfunctional family and I'll spend many more. It isn't all that hard, because we don't speak to each other anymore. Many of us are dead, drunk, or insane. Sometimes it's like that, and I have come to understand and accept this. I've learned to throw out the bad and cling to the good, and I've learned not to pretend it was all good. I've learned it is impossible to go back and recreate a new ending, and I've learned to keep things in context and look at the big picture. This works for me.

Tinkerbell died in 1976 and Mama died in 1987. I miss them

both. I miss Tinkerbell when I realize there's nowhere to run and hide, and I miss Mama when *As the World Turns* comes on. I miss her whenever I see a patchwork quilt, and I miss her when I water my pink impatiens, her favorite flower. Every spring, I vow not to plant any more impatiens, but I always end up with basket after basket, pot after pot and flowerbed after flowerbed of red, white, fuchsia, coral, lavender, and pink blossoms. I keep glasses full of impatiens on my windowsill, constantly rooting and perpetuating new growth.

Purple hull peas and cornbread remind me of Mama, along with asparagus casserole and iced tea with lemon. Front porch swings, white flower boxes, and Chanel No. 5 bring her back. So do tiny pink rosebuds, fresh Folgers coffee, orange pound cake, and old-fashioned flip-flops, or clod-hoppers, as she called them. I smile at the memory of a small Coke in a glass bottle, Breck shampoo, and pink foam hair curlers. Mama especially liked these, because they provided her with the perfect excuse for sending me into the grocery to buy her L&Ms. Of course, no one knew Mama smoked. It was unladylike.

"Everything reminds you of your mother," my daughter says, rolling her eyes. I tell her it's like that when you miss someone.

When Mama died, a family friend threw her arms around me and said, "Nobody loves you like your mama." She was right. At the time, I thought it was just one of those things people say when they don't know what to say. Now I realize truer words were never spoken.

When my babies were born, especially the boy babies, I wanted my mama. We only had girls in the house I grew up in, and I was clueless about the cleansing of certain body parts. My maternal experiences were limited to Betsy Wetsy and Chatty Cathy, who both ended up headless and nude.

When my boss made me cry, I wanted my Mama. She would have chewed him up and spit him out, because she was the only person on earth who was allowed to make me cry. When Mama got mad, "ladylike" when down the drain. She could flat ruffle some feathers.

Whenever I hear "Abide with Me," I want my mama, and if I were prone to drink, "Abba Dabba Honeymoon" would send me straight to the liquor cabinet. Mama used to get a wild hair and sing that crazy song, while she danced like a Billy goat and slung a grandbaby around.

Yes, I do miss my mama. I always will.

11. From Blue to Green

It's graduation time again – that time of life when we look at our children and wonder when they went from chocolate bunnies to prom dresses, and from Hot Wheels to Mustangs.

Somehow it's easier for me to look back rather than forward. At least I know what's back there.

My daughter graduates this year, my firstborn.

When she was three, I had the talk with her about not "talking to people she didn't know." That very day, she disappeared and the whole neighborhood was out looking for her. I found her out hiding in the storage shed.

"What in the world are you doing out here?" I screamed. "You scared me to death!"

"I was hiding from all the people I didn't know," she replied.

Later that year, I signed her up for preschool in the fall. Ever the independent and confident child, I was surprised when she wavered at the end. I took her to the bathroom and her little chin trembled. "Will I be just fine?" she asked.

"Yes, you'll be just fine," I said.

The next year, as I was pounding the rules of "yes ma'am and no ma'am" into her hard Southern head, she made an astute observation. My husband was standing in a chair, painting the walls of his new home office.

"Do you what a ham sandwich for lunch?" I asked.

"Yes," he replied.

"Poor old Daddy," my little one said. "He doesn't even say 'yes ma'am.'"

That was the same year my mother died. For reasons unknown, my daughter called her grandmother "Urdula." One sunshiny day in early May, my mother carried her outside to look at the flowers. "Urdula would you turn out that light?" she asked.

Everything happens in May. Later that month I got the call.

"Something's happened to Mother," my sister said. "They've life flighted her to the hospital."

My daughter packed her little yellow Care Bears suitcase. "I know God's phone number," she said to me.

When my daughter was thirteen she turned into a vegetarian and I had to lure her back to reality with a chicken breast.

When she turned sixteen I experienced true hatred for boys and begged her to become a nun or a lesbian.

Now she's eighteen and I've tried every trick in the book. I hope she still has God's phone number, and I hope and pray that she will "be just fine."

She's painting the walls of her bedroom for her brother to move into. From blue to green, she'll be gone. Just like that.

When they told me it was this hard, I didn't believe them. When I thought I knew how to let go, I was wrong. So often in life, we have no choice. If we did, would we ever let go? Probably not.

I pray that I can make it through "Pomp and Circumstance" without anyone having to call an ambulance. Surely I can do this.

I've always cried more at high school graduations than at weddings or even funerals. There is more separation anxiety in the air at a high school graduation than any other event in life. The ambivalence of clinging mixed with the exhilaration of letting go presents an emotional roller coaster. But like any thrill ride, there is a sense of satisfaction and relief at the end. There is even the desire to do it all over again.

I'm ready for that relief and that satisfaction. I've been standing in this line for eighteen years and the last two weeks have seemed the longest. It's time to buckle up, turn fifteen flips and get jerked around like a tree in a tornado.

Will I be just fine? I think so. If not, I still have God's phone number.

12. Change of Venue

On a hazy August morn in the mid-seventies, I was college bound. My flight was scheduled to leave at 11:00 A.M., and I had the jitters. This was the biggest transition I'd ever made – goodbye to friends, parents, grandparents, and my hometown. Plus, I was going to have to give up smoking because smoking was banned at this college. "Oh, well," I told myself. "I'll cross that bridge when come to it." Yeah, I crossed that bridge, all right, about ten minutes after touchdown. Smokers, like other drug addicts, have a gift for scouting each other out and finding great smoking hideouts. There is a dangerous recognition in addiction.

I have thought of that August morn many times. My parents were downstairs, spazzed out and scurrying around like hyped-up Coneheads. My father had irrational fears of being late to the airport, and my mother tended to chain smoke and twirl around in circles whenever she got nervous. Our family could have easily been called "The Frightened Family," but that's another story.

I remember climbing the steps to my bedroom one last time and sitting down on my bed. I'd lived there for years and never seen it in that way – *The Wizard of Oz* on the bookshelf, the window seat with a great view of the walnut trees on our downtown street, the built-in chest of drawers with socks and t-shirts hanging out of it. The bottle of Mateus on my windowsill with a melted candle stuck inside. The pewter piggy bank my best friend had given me for my sixteenth birthday. James Taylor's "Sweet Baby James" staring up at me from the floor, reminding me that at least the song and its memories would remain the same.

I sat on the bed and noticed that everything seemed still, as if the moment were frozen in time. It was a new sensation – one I later felt the night my mother died – and one I am feeling right now.

It's called change. I sat on that bed, aware that if I didn't get out of there soon, my parents would have simultaneous heart attacks. But I took a long look around, knowing that when I returned, things would never be the same. It's like that when you go away to college.

My daughter leaves today, and I know that when I walk into her room, that same stillness will be in the air. There will be childhood pictures left on the dresser, and flowers left in the vase. She'll leave books and clothes strewn on the floor, but they'll be remnants of a life well spent; one that has already accomplished much. She'll move on and she'll do well, but things will never be the same.

I recently spotted a bottle of Mateus and envisioned a dripping candle sticking out of the top. "It would look perfect on my windowsill!" I told my husband, who had that "whatever you say" look on his face. For the life of me, I couldn't understand why he didn't get excited about a candle sticking out of a bottle of Mateus. "Do you know how long it's been since I've seen this stuff?" I asked him. "I thought it was extinct!"

He popped the cork a couple of days later and turned up his nose like a pig in a slaughterhouse. "Skanky," he said.

I turned on "Free Bird" and turned up my wine glass, anxious to re-live my seventies moments. After a few sips, I had to admit the best thing about Mateus was the candle stuck in the top. Life is full of realizations, some slow and some sudden.

Here's a toast to the future, with all its uncertainties, and to the moments of our pasts, when time taps us on the shoulder and makes us stand still.

13. Girl Scout Trauma

hen I was little, I would stand on a kitchen chair and eat sugar by the spoonful, straight out of the sugar bowl.

"Get out of that sugar bowl, girl!" my mother would yell, and I would down one more lovin' spoonful.

I would leap out of the chair, put my hands on my hips and proclaim, "When I grow up I'm going to buy a whole pound of sugar and eat it all by myself."

My mother, ever the unnerved one, would just stare at me in fear of what I would do next.

I grew up, Mama died, and I never ate that pound of sugar because adulthood somehow squelched the desire.

People say things have changed, and in many ways they have. As a child, I spent my summer days with my friends at the pool and the adjoining park. Back then they didn't have cameras in parks because the only people there were screaming, barefoot kids eating Boston Baked Beans and Sweet Tarts and large wads of Bazooka Bubble Gum.

These days, you can't even pick your nose in the park or adjust your wedgie, due to certain unmentionable acts.

Yes, things have changed but that's not to say that past generations were unscathed.

Ironically, it was the Girl Scout experience that traumatized me most. It was bad enough having to flounce around in the green Girl Scout dress with the sash. It was cute back in the Brownie years, but my green sash was lacking in badges and I never could find my pins.

Oh, if only it had stopped there in the midst of the lame, but my Girl Scout years were the end of my innocence. It could all be summed up by the title "Rita Does Freddie Krueger."

One fateful Friday night back in fifth grade, our Girl Scout leaders held a sleepover for us at our regular meeting place, which included a kitchen and several other rooms. The leaders were snoring away by 10:00 P.M. and we had free reign. For weeks, Rita had been promising to tell us "the facts of life," and we eagerly awaited the moment. Rita, at age eleven, was somehow the hormonal equivalent of a 21-year-old.

On the floor of the tiny kitchen, we all gathered wide-eyed around Rita, perched on the ledge of the facts of life. Still being the child who planned to eat a whole pound of sugar when I grew up, I had no idea what the facts of life entailed.

Rita proceeded to tell us in great detail about how she and the preacher's boy often went down underneath the bridge in the tall green grass. Most of the girls seemed impressed, but I was unable to grasp the notion. There was simply no way to integrate such a tale with my dream of eating a pound of sugar.

Around midnight, we gathered round while Rita stood in the middle of a circle, snapping her fingers and singing Roger Miller's "King of the Road." I have never recovered from that night, and I now know why they need cameras in parks and trolls underneath bridges.

And then there was the time they took us to the county jail and we saw an encaged woman who thought she was a bird and was squawking and flapping her arms. I'll admit, this was without question the highlight of my Girl Scout years.

There was much, much more, but enough is enough.

Suffice it to say I never forced my own daughters to be Girl Scouts. I let them play video games and eat sugar instead.

14. Mild Obcenity

And now I'd like to thank the would-be obscene caller who phoned my house a few days ago, for turning an otherwise mundane afternoon into a challenging and beneficial exercise. He's a mere "would-be," because I slammed the phone down before he got to the good stuff. Mama always said hanging up was the proper etiquette when handling an obscene phone caller, although her preferred method was the cowbell.

Back in the late sixties, an obscene phone caller took a hankering to Mama. He'd call, and she'd sit there on her kitchen stool with a cigarette dangling from her lip while examining the toenails on her right foot. She'd wedge the black telephone receiver between her shoulder and her ear, looking preoccupied but slightly amused. Eventually, a look of disgust would crawl across her face, and she'd turn beet red and slam the phone down like it was on fire. Sadly, Mama never revealed the words her caller uttered to her because they probably weren't "ladylike." As was so often the case, she did not follow her own advice, and instead clung to the weasel's every word. I suppose intrigue made her do it, or perhaps boredom. One day, upon the slamming down of the phone, she had a light bulb moment. "I'm going to get that fool," she hissed, "if it's the last thing I do!"

A couple of days later, the phone rang. My sisters and I watched our mother go through the usual rituals of the obscene phone call, then watched in horror as she grabbed a cowbell and rang it into the phone for what seemed an eternity. The phone caller never rang again, and we never knew his identity. Oddly enough, the preacher began wearing a hearing aid shortly after the incident.

Mamas have such a huge influence on their children. Here I am, faced with the same dilemma that plagued my own Mama so many years ago, and instead of doing the right thing and hanging up the phone, I long to take the road not taken and do something bizarre. I can't help it.

I've been thinking about some possible alternatives to simply hanging up the phone. Next time, when he gets to the part where he rasps, "Do you want to know what I'm doing?" I could respond with these comebacks:

• Praying?
• No, but I'm sure my husband would. Here, talk to him.
• Let's see…I'll bet you're reading *Beowulf.*
• Don't tell me -- you're painting the Sistine Chapel ceiling!
• You don't have to tell me what you're doing. I work for the FBI and I'm watching every move you make. We all are.
• I'd bet money you're watching "The Power Puff Girls.
• I don't know what you're doing, but I'm fondling a cleaver."

I've always heard obscene phone callers are harmless cowards who rarely act on their words. Not only am I appalled by their motives, I am amazed they have somehow found the time to engage in such stupidity. Is this their goal in life? And I wonder, what does a 90-year-old obscene phone caller sound like? Does he use speed dial? Or does he give up this practice in his rocking chair years and simply reminisce about the good old days?

So many questions, so few answers … I may have to seek some expert advice on the matter. On the other hand, I may just get out the cowbell and ring that ding-a-ling all the way to the moon.

15. Mother's Day

We're well into May, the month of motherhood and roses. May is also the month in which my mother both arrived and departed from this world. For those of us who have lost our mothers, Mother's Day can be bittersweet. It can be a reminder of what we once had, and it can be a reminder of things we will never have.

What makes a good mother? Is it a clean house? Is it the absence of marital spats in a family? Is it warm chocolate chip cookies fresh from the oven, or apple pie with whipped cream on top?

Above all, I believe a good mother is one who reveals the truth to her children. Good mothers, for example, do not forever pretend their husbands are faithful "for the sake of the children." Good mothers do not protect abusive men out of fear of being alone. Good mothers do not live in fear of "what the neighbors think." Good mothers adjust to their teenagers' hatred of them, and learn to view it as a good sign. Good mothers face the music when the notes turn sour. Good mothers seek forgiveness when the need arises, and they do not take it for granted. Good mothers learn from their mistakes and forgive themselves, and they pick their friends and arguments wisely. Mothers turn houses into homes.

Home is the place where the deal was done. We all emerge from that place in some form, and some deals are better than others. One thing's for sure, though. The mothers are the ones who shake on the deals. Mothers are powerful because they are women, and women are the most powerful beings on earth because of three little words: yes, no and maybe. Simply put, men are easy. Motherhood, however, is not. Motherhood travels back and forth from Heaven to Hell, sometimes at the speed of light.

"What do you want for Mother's Day?" my husband asks.

"Nothing, really," I say, in a rare moment of silence. As my husband recently pointed out to me, "In the dictionary beside the word 'subtle,' your name ain't there." But my husband can't give me what I want for Mother's Day. He helped make me a mother, and that alone is enough. Still I am human and I am nostalgic and I long for things I cannot have.

I want to hear my mother say, "Do you have plenty of money?" "Are you getting enough to eat?" "What did you learn at school today?" I want to sit on her front porch and smell the petunias after a rain. I want to drink a cup of coffee with her at the small green kitchen table, and I want to eat just one more piece of her fried chicken.

My mother was a rare blend, somewhere between June Cleaver and Bette Davis. I remember the last time I ever saw my mother. I was backing out of her driveway and she was waving goodbye to me and smiling. Somehow, I think she still is.

16. My Mother

 nd now, for the millionth time, I will write about the missing piece otherwise known as my mother.

"Why do you feel so strongly about your mother?" my friend asks. "Was it her approval you wanted, or what?"

Hah. I would have never gotten her approval. It was her appeal, her entertainment value. The lure of the old clapboard house in town, with its big front porch and white columns. The small chipped green kitchen table, one that I might now find in a Mississippi antique store, due to its authenticity. The pink scuffs: "Hon, have you seen my pink scuffs?" The Drixoral: "Hon, would you get me a Drixoral? My head is about to kill me!"

Something was always about to kill her. "I do believe you girls will kill me!" she often told my sisters and me. And if it didn't nearly kill her, it came close: "I do not believe I can stand it if she stays a whole week!" she would say, regarding a certain relative from Cincinnati.

And many things, including her in-laws, would nearly drive her insane: "I do believe they will drive me insane!" she often said. "He disgusts me to the core, ambling along like a big old rhinoceros!"

The smell of her cigarettes, lit up with her Folgers in the morning, enticed me. I miss my mornings with Mama, perched on the kitchen stool beside the red telephone -- Mama scuffing around getting nothing accomplished – a plate here, a saucer there; merely rearranging the chaos.

"Hon, you want some toast?" she'd ask, as it popped up out of the toaster and into the air, and before I could even say no, she'd be flinging it in front of me on a saucer, like a Frisbee to a dog.

"No, I don't think so," I'd say, but she'd never hear me because she'd be mesmerized by Bill Hall, or watching out the window for her daddy, just in case he came in and caught her smoking. My mother lived much of her life on the verge of having to put out a cigarette.

I thought I was over her. I have recently concluded I will never be over her.

It was her quirky elitism that no one outside the family knew of -- elitism I can't even put into words: "But I can't wear these!" she once screamed at my older sister, over a pair of black designer pumps at Christmas, chunking them under the tree like a child who'd gotten the wrong Barbie Doll.

Mama was something akin to Aunt Bee meets Norman Bates, or Bette Davis meets June Cleaver. On her worst days, she was Bette Davis meets Norman Bates.

Always entertaining, never easy to define. Loved to quilt by hand with her two close friends, adored her flowers, especially pink impatiens: "Hon, look at this one – it looks just like a baby girl's face!"

My sisters and I would roll our eyes at her original sayings, such as "I'm tired as a rat!" and "If you act as nice as you look, you'll do just fine."

Mama was a hypocrite, yet she hated pretense or hypocrisy. For this reason, we attended church three times a week and shook hands with the preachers and elders whom we mocked back home in the kitchen where we smoked our brains out. And there at church, we hugged the grandparents with whom Mama maintained a steady internal struggle – the old 'smile- on your face, knife in your back' type deal.

It never occurred to me that I would actually try to understand such things.

Sometimes Mama wore Gloria Vanderbilt perfume. When she died in 1987, I found myself spraying a whiff or two into the room, just to be near her once again.

Logical people might ask, "But why would you want to be near her once again? Why can't you just rock that old baby to sleep?"

But the heart is sometimes an illogical thing, and still I crave her.

It's been sixteen years since my mother died. I often wonder how it would be if she could see me now, for I have changed. I do not rearrange chaos ; I throw it away. I don't fool others or myself with a smile or a knife. I don't smoke, but I do love Bill Hall and I'm thankful he's still around.

It's funny. I have a pair of pink house shoes, or "scuffs," as Mama said, that I sometimes wear. When I put them on and walk across my wood floor, the sound is inimitable: it is the sound of my mother, scuffing all over the place, permanently and genetically encoded into my being. It is a deep, deep thing; deeper than any ocean. It is the love of my mother, with all her mysterious waters, in which I will eternally swim.

P**A**RT iii

Nostalgia: Running With Scissors Down Memory Lane

1. A House in Town

It was a house in town – white clapboard, black shutters, large white columns, and an old white swing, waiting for someone to sit down and set it into motion. A small bare-footed child, pushing herself higher into the air, bursting with giggles of delight and glee that only a small child can emit. And her mother, stooped over her white flowerboxes, filled with pink impatiens and white petunias, slightly annoyed with root rot and her daughter's dusty feet, yet smiling at life in spite of it all. The mother had a gift for that.

Later, the swing moved gently back and forth, soothing the broken hearts of adolescence, and enhancing first kisses in honeysuckle breezes.

Later still, the swing lulled our own babies to sleep as we swung back and forth, watching the cars and our lives go by.

I miss that house in town.

Sometimes I drive by and look at the empty flowerboxes, the motionless swing, and my heart aches at the contrast of life and death; past and present. My mother is dead, but the memory is not.

In my teenage years, I would sit out on my porch, prop my dusty bare feet up against the columns, and smoke my Marlboro 100's. Even then, I suspected there was nothing better than vegging out in my front porch rocking chair, smoking cigarettes and staring into space. I miss the luxury of being goal-free and brain dead.

I am thankful to have once had the opportunity to embrace that state of mind. I am thankful, too, that I was later able to quit smoking and move on with my life. Yet sometimes I am drawn to the memory of my childhood home and the lure of that swing, now sitting cold and empty like the flowerboxes. I want to sit in it once more and feel my dusty bare feet slide across the coolness of the porch. I want to listen to the tired old creak of the chains that hold me. I want the flowerboxes to bloom again, with rainbows of impatiens spilling over the sides. I want to prop my feet back up on that column and forget about life for a while. I want an unsure kiss in the honeysuckle breeze, but most of all, I want my Mama.

What is it about a mama that makes us miss them so? When my mama was alive, I didn't even like her, much less appreciate her. And even in death, I have not immortalized her, as we often do the deceased. Like all of us, my mama had lots of flaws. She yelled too much, she smoked too much, and she built her very existence on *As the World Turns*. The house could have been engulfed in flames, and she wouldn't have budged if Bob and Lisa had been locked in an embrace. There was always the slightest of possibilities they would reunite, and if they ever do, I am confident my mother will rise up from the dead.

I believe it is the comfort of home that makes us miss our mamas. Until it is too late, we often don't realize what we had was a little better than we wanted to admit.

This Thanksgiving, let your mama know you love her, even if she drives you insane. Accept her flaws and seek her perfections, for all mamas have areas of perfection. Any mama, no matter what she has ever done, deserves a round of applause for sticking around during her offspring's teenage years.

Rake her leaves, buy her a new dress, or give her some flowers. Thank her for giving you life. And if you have the opportunity to sit in an old swing on an old front porch, take off your shoes, sail too high, and hold on tight.

2. Tabu

othing conjures up a whiff of the past like the sense of smell.

Aside from destroying thousands of brain cells, a sniff of Tabu perfume takes me back to my eighth grade year. Tabu was dark, heavy and thick, and could strip the membranes from a nose in three seconds flat. My older sisters stashed it away in the bathroom cabinet, right beside the Emeraude, the Arpege and My Sin. No wonder my mother anguished over her daughters, with the lascivious potion they were dabbing behind their ears.

And then the pristine White Shoulders came along, in an apparent attempt to preserve the purity of the sixties girls, but who were they kidding? The delicate Victorian lure of White Shoulders led more teens to Lovers Lane than Tabu ever dreamed of. One whiff of White Shoulders, and my sisters' drooling dates scooped them up in their arms and whisked them away, like any true knight would do.

No, desire wasn't truly squelched until the designer collections made their debut. These perfumes consisted of a mere name: Bill Blass, Calvin Klein, Liz Claiborne, and Ralph Lauren. Sure, they smelled OK, and they were certainly trendy, but the passion was not in the bottle. Tabu, be it ever so heavy, would take you there, all the way to desperate searches for hicky-hiding turtlenecks, and sometimes all the way to the delivery room.

I received my early lessons in love from watching behind the scenes. I viewed these clandestine scenes from a chair in my bedroom, where I would stand on tiptoe and stare into the mirror above the mantel in the living room, which was conveniently located in front of the happening place, otherwise known as the couch. It was great stuff, yet sometimes predictable. My oldest sister would sit there with her boyfriend, reeking of Tabu and staring into his pleading eyes. Then they would kiss and tenderly place their hands on each others' cheeks and ever so slowly but oh so predictably, would slide out of view, into a semi-reclining position on the arm of the couch.

The middle sister, interestingly, would do the same thing as the older sister. Were they genetically programmed to gaze, kiss, touch cheeks and recline? Where was their sense of creativity and adventure? It was obvious they had watched way too many episodes of *All My Children*.

I wanted some real action. Just once, I wanted my mother to dash out of her bedroom in her pink sponge hair curlers and Pond's cold cream slathered on her face. I wanted my father to lunge out with his hair sticking up like a troll on Brylcreem and say, "Just what are you two doing out here? Is there a sign that says 'orgy' in our living room? And young lady, what's that blob on your neck? I don't recall you being born with a pond-shaped birthmark!"

And then my sister would plead, "It was the *Tabu*, Daddy. "We just couldn't help ourselves. Please don't be mad at us! We were under the spell!"

And then, in a simple twist of fate, my father could have leaned over to my mother and whispered, "Where the hell does she keep that stuff?"

It could have happened.

3. Hometown Grocery Store

There's a certain grocery store in town that is authentic. It is the kind of store where my mother shopped, and it is a special and dying breed. The demise of the hometown grocery store would make a great political cause. If we saved that damned mussel, we can certainly save this precious pearl.

This store boasts no plastic savings card or triple coupons. They don't give away free trips to Hawaii, and they don't sell beer. They do have great specials and the best meat department in town.

Stroll down the aisles and you might see a little old lady in a red felt hat with a feather on top. She'll carry a little black pocketbook, and she will buy three or four small items; perhaps bread, milk and a mess of fresh green beans.

There's the angelic employee who's been there forever, and addresses many patrons as "darlin'," "sweetheart," or "baby."

"And how are you today, sweetheart?" she asks, as she scans my groceries with a care that is unheard of in this day and age. And she means it when she calls me sweetheart, in a good kind of way. This gal cares. She takes time to talk to the little old lady in the feathered cap, not because she has to, but because she wants to, and because she know she might be the only person who talks to her that day.

She says things like, "How are you today, Miss Emma? You feeling better this week? We missed you at church yesterday."

I'll bet this employee has added fifteen years to Miss Emma's life, and made the store a ton of money to boot.

The old-timey smells in this grocery store carry me back to

my childhood. It's different in here. When I walk by the Keebler Elf cookies, their sweetness almost melts in my mouth. Get a whiff of the Nabisco vanilla wafers and Zesta saltines. There is no specialty deli, and that's good. A deli would cheapen this place.

Back in the meat department, smells of ham bring back memories of huge country breakfasts. Over in produce, the turnip greens are healthy, fresh and reminiscent of a Southern feast, complete with fresh tomatoes and fried corn.

The Moon Pies are reserved on a special throne, over by the bread, and the small cans of snuff are adorable. I like to look at them, all neatly lined up in their little red and white tins. My 93- year-old great-grandmother liked to look at them, too.

Yet another comfort of this hometown grocery store is the familiar faces. It's nice to see people you know, or knew ten or fifteen years ago. It's nice to hear conversations like this one:

"And how's your sister doing, Louise?"

"Oh, not a bit good. She's got the shingles and she's mean as a snake. I came here to get her some Gold Bond Powder and to get out of the house for a little bit."

Or this one...

"You should see my Bradford Pears, Marie. Best trees this side of Texas."

"You're always bragging about something or other, Henry. Bradford pears smell like dead fish. You don't even own a tulip poplar, and if you don't like tulip poplars, you ain't worth squat!"

I couldn't care less about coupons, bonus points, plastic cards, new grocery carts and mega-sized aisles. Just give me bagboys with white aprons and unpierced ears, old-fashioned brown bags, and an array of parsnips.

Let's preserve the old-time grocery store. Write your congressman today.

4. Wringer Washing Machine

Recently my husband and I stopped at a Cracker Barrel in Jackson, Tennessee, after visiting a fun place in the Delta Region. I ate my usual buttermilk pancakes and he ate his usual Big Boy Cardiovascular Country Sampler, and we left the restaurant. As we walked by the nostalgic memorabilia in front of the store, I spotted a wringer washing machine and surprised even my own self by bursting into tears. "Oh, look at that wringer washing machine!" I blurted, both laughing and crying at the same time.

"It's OK, honey," said my husband, also laughing at the un-expected nature of the outburst. "I know what it means to you."

I know what it means to me, too. A few years ago when the family farm was auctioned off after my grandparent's deaths, their house was torn down and I wrote this true story about my granny and her wringer washing machine. I have come to realize my experience had nothing at all to do with the wringer washing machine, and everything to do with a grandmother's love.

ॐ ॐ ॐ ॐ ॐ

I am a child, seven or eight years old. It is mid-June, and I am spending two weeks with my maternal grandparents.

Outside, the grass is wet with dew and the humidity is high. It is around nine o'clock, and I am goofing around in the yard. I go look at the Black Angus cows through the fence. They look back at me with dull, blank expressions in their eyes, and then walk away. They do not know me.

I go to the front yard and examine the trees. The pear tree is loaded with tiny green pears, and the walnut tree over in the corner has lemon-shaped walnuts on it. The other walnut trees are normal.

I walk back to the kitchen door and turn to see a truck pulling in. It comes up the long gravel drive and parks in front of the house. Two men climb out, let the tailgate down, and unload a large box.

Perplexed, I go in the house and tell Granny two men are bringing a large box up the driveway.

Granny steps outside and smiles. "Right in here," she says.

"All rightey, Ma'am," the men say. "We'll fix her right up."

In no time, they have installed a brand new washing machine on Granny's back porch. It is white, shiny and square, and fits perfectly into the corner. Granny sets a box of Cheer on top and beams.

They roll out Granny's old wringer washer, load it onto their truck, and drive away. Just like that, it is gone.

I go into the bathroom, confused. What is happening to me? Why can't I stop crying? This is stupid! They took away the wringer washing machine and my heart is breaking. Granny and I used to have so much fun with that washing machine. She put the clothes in and I pulled them out. That was enough for me.

Granny gently opens the door and sees my tears. I feel ashamed.

"What's wrong, hon?" She asks.

"Nothing," I say. "I'm OK."

Granny does not push me, and I offer no more explanation. But she knows. She knows and understands much more deeply than I do.

Through the years, Granny makes an occasional, sweet reference to the day I cried when they took away the wringer washer. She mentions it to my mother, and she mentions it to me.

She doesn't mention it often, though, because she knows I will cry all over again. Granny respects my feelings, and that is why I love her so.

May every child be so blessed.

5. The Box

y sister and I have been cleaning out old boxes of memorabilia.

She found a letter I'd written seventeen years ago when I was barely pregnant with my second child: "I'm sure it's just nerves," it read. "The job's pretty stressful right now and all. Besides, there's no way I could be pregnant...no way at all. Why, I don't even sleep anymore – I stay up all night sterilizing bottles and checking on the baby. Come to think of it, I haven't seen "Carl" in six months."

Turned out to be an 8 lb., 11 oz. nerve with cute little dimples and eyes like saucers.

I scrounged around in the box some more and found a picture of myself five minutes after giving birth to the third bundle of nerves. This being the birth where the epidural did not work, the photo could have easily been captioned "Linda Blair with Rabies."

Pregnant women do strange things. At the end of my fourth pregnancy, my cousin, who was also a labor and delivery nurse, took a profile shot of my stomach. This lovely portrait could have qualified me as the poster girl for Planned Parenthood.

In my collection of memories, I ran across letters from old flames. There was the poem entitled "Nectar," written by my pseudo-intellectual boyfriend who later left me for divinity school. I read "Nectar" for the first time in years, and an image flashed through my head: I'm chasing a scrawny baby around the couch with a Flintstone vitamin, while Socrates is obsessively squeezing out a poem called "Stamen. "

Glad that one didn't work out.

I ran across snippets from Mama. My mother, *As the World Turns* aficionado, didn't write letters. She scratched notes on the covers of match books: I think Bob and Lisa are about to get back together. – November 3, 1969

Mama also waxed eloquent on the backs of pictures. On the back of my fifth grade piano recital picture she wrote, "Better enjoy this time of your life – your nose will never be this small again."

Of all the wonders in the world, my mother was most impressed by the fact that our noses never stopped growing. Admittedly, the nose information made such an impression on me that I have passed this knowledge down to my children. When he was five, my fourth child asked, "Mama, if my nose sticks up out of the ground after I'm buried, will they run over it with the lawnmower?"

"No, baby," I reassured him. "If it's decorated with ivy and a miniature rose bush, no one will touch it."

In my treasure chest from the past, "the box" ranks highest among the collection. "The box" is my miniature Lane cedar chest that I got from a local furniture store when I graduated from high school.

It takes something monumental to make the box. There's a picture of my grandparents smiling in front of their hibiscus bush that is bursting with big red blooms. There is a miniature paper parasol from my first mixed drink. There are two "Jimmy Carter for President" buttons. There's a picture of Tinkerbell, our 14-year-old poodle who had her own personal gourmet chef. There's the birth announcement from when I was born.

There is the basketball schedule from my eighth grade year, along with a picture of our team. And there is my most prized possession – a snippet of Thomasina's cat hair inside a miniature Cornsilk compact.

This keepsake failed to tug at my husband's heartstrings.

"You're one sick puppy," he said.

"You're just jealous because you didn't save any of Smoky's hair," I replied. "If I die before you, make sure this goes in the Museum of the Greatest Cats of the twenty-first Century."

"Give me that box," he said, thumbing through it hungrily. "Where am I?" Why didn't I make the box?"

"It takes twenty years to make the box," I said. "I haven't known you that long."

It's been over nineteen years. In less than two months, he's going to flood the box.

Anyone out there have a spare?

6. Falling off the Pony

Back when my husband and I got married, there was no Oprah or Dr. Phil. We did have Donohue, who was in the experimental stages of exposing marital woes to the world, and during our honeymoon phase we had no inkling of marital woes so we did not watch Donahue. We watched Ralph Emory's Channel 4 early morning show, complete with absence of psychological trauma, and back then that was plenty for us.

But issues and differences soon erupted, sometimes on a Mount St. Helen's or an Asian tsunami level, and this was baffling, for my husband and I could not locate the epicenter of our marital storms. After years of research and development, I finally determined the cause: Men and women are different, and most of our differences lie in communication. Women talk while men stare at the TV.

Conan O'Brien recently quoted, "A study in *The Washington Post* says that women have better verbal skills than men. I just want to say to the authors of that study: 'Duh.'"

Luckily, my husband and I have been able to work through our differences for the most part, and have found creative solutions to the things that drive me crazy, for I am the one who is always driven crazy because my husband *accepts* things and I do not. I attribute this trait of his to his earliest memory, when at the age of three he was sitting on the back of a truck atop a stack of hay and farm implements, when suddenly a hog with a slit throat was tossed upon him, bleeding and dead. He looked at the hog and processed the experience quickly and said to himself, "Hmmm ... so this is the way life is. OK, I'll deal with this carnage for the next fifteen years and live on the farm in peace with my parents, and then I'll get the hell out of Dodge." And that is exactly what he did.

My earliest memory involved being led by my uncle in a horse show in the rain. I was wearing my little crimson riding breeches, perched atop a pony named Baby Doll, when suddenly I became aware that I was falling off the pony in slow motion. "I'm falling off the pony," I whispered to my uncle, who just smiled and waved at the crowd as we circled the ring. It got worse. "I'm falling off the pony!" I said, this time louder.

But still he smiled and waved and clinched his teeth and said, 'Hold on, gal – we're gonna win this thing.' The inevitable happened: I fell off the pony and went splat in the mud, yet somehow managed to win the blue ribbon, which made my uncle proud. Yet the moment resulted in my going through life with the feeling that I was falling off the pony, crying for help, while no one listened because of his own agendas.

Two different experiences that became metaphors for our lives – the epicenter of our marital storms. My husband has realized that I may not readily accept life's harsh realities, and I have learned to jump off the pony and run for my life when I am in danger. And blue ribbons and trophies and diplomas mean nothing to me – you will not see them hung on my wall or displayed in a case.

And although it is clear in my mind, you won't see the picture of a little girl in red riding breeches, mad and confused, who learned to turn her anger into something good and rescue herself.

7. Seasons of the Past

here's a hint of fall in the air that makes me reminiscent of the summer of my eighteenth year. I get this way every year.

I was going away to a "church college" in September, and it was the summer of the big blowout. Back then, I had an all-or-nothing mentality that ironically, had developed in church. I was like the binge eater who polishes off one last bag of Oreos before the initial Weight Watchers meeting. I smoked a generous supply of Marlboro 100s, spent my nights with friends, drinking beer through straws and circling around Sonic, once wearing duck masks.

One night in particular stands out, and it is only now that I understand why. One of my best friends lived across from the old football stadium – the best high school football stadium in the country. Never mind the fact that we had only seen ten others. There were three of us – all Leos – and we had been friends for years. We were old friends who seemed to know each other better than we knew ourselves. At eighteen, anything's possible.

It was the middle of August at two in the morning, and the town was asleep. We slipped out of my friend's house and walked over to the football field where we'd spent many a night cheering in the crowd and chasing after boys. The seats were empty and the field was dark, and we walked down to the goal post and sat down. We had been drinking beer through straws and eating Fritos and peanut M & M's, and we were laughing about old times. Back then, we had code names for people –

Nose Picker, Squirrel Teeth, and Blowfish, to name a few. We were close friends and we spoke our own special language, as best friends so often do.

I remember that night on the football field, not because of any monumental event, but because we suddenly got up and ran. We ran and ran and ran, laughing all the way, telling stories about Nose Picker and Squirrel Teeth and Blowfish, until we collapsed at the other end of the field and stared up at the stars. No one mentioned the future because the acknowledgement was too scary. We were in the throes of regression, holding onto the past – uncertain of the future – in a most memorable way.

When I go to the swimming pool this time of year, I am re-minded of a hazy day in August in the summer of my eighteenth year. I was in the middle of the swimming pool, sitting on an inner tube with a boy who was merely a friend, and it started to rain. The crowd was sparse, and I sensed it was different that year. People and friends had started to scatter like leaves in the wind; blowing in all different directions. Some would blow away forever, never to return home. Some would go to New York and pursue acting careers, and some would stay home and marry their high school sweethearts, only to desperately search for their youth twenty years down the road.

You can't go home again but you can die trying.

Life is funny. I went to the church school and stayed for three weeks. The all-or-nothing mentality got the best of me, and it took me twenty years to be glad.

I don't cruise around Sonic anymore in a duck mask, and I don't run up and down the football field in the middle of the night. I no longer smoke, and I rarely see the old friends who once knew me better than I knew myself.

I live in the present and look forward to the future, because I have learned to be thankful for the seasons of my past.

8. Heaven

What's Heaven like?' my precocious child once asked me. "Are the streets really gold? Is Saint Peter really standing at the Pearly Gates with the Book of Life in his hands? Do they really keep up with every single thing I ever do in my entire life?"

"I don't know, honey, but just in case, why don't you be a good girl and take out the trash, clean your room, wash the dishes and walk the dog?"

Fear and doubt do have their advantages. Heaven. What *is* it really like?

Songs have been sung and movies made about Heaven such as "No Tears in Heaven," *Tears in Heaven, Ghost* and *Heaven Can Wait*. Many jokes have been made about Heaven, because we tend to joke about our greatest fears.

Whenever we think of Heaven, words like God, Jesus, utopia, clouds, angels, saints, eternity, blue skies, streets of gold and Pearly Gates come to mind.

Studies show that an overwhelming majority of people not only believe in Heaven, they think they will go there when they die. And while some people believe there's a red devil wagging his tail, complete with horns and pitchfork, just waiting to skewer evildoers over the red-hot coals of eternity, the Devil is something that happens to other people.

I believe Heaven is a place where the kitchen drawers slide open without falling off their hinges. The blades on the ceiling fan are clean, and faucets never drip. Mama is there, bent over her green-chipped kitchen table, working the crossword puzzle, drinking a cup of Folgers and planning her day around *As the World Turns*. Outside on her front porch, impatiens spill over the sides of the white flowerboxes her daddy built for her.

Yes, there is a front porch in Heaven, with a swing and a barefoot girl with dusty feet who is laughing and swinging way too high.

Maybe it's a place where it feels good even when the bees sting.

I believe Heaven is a place where all has been forgiven and nothing bad exists, and I believe we catch glimpses of it right here on earth.

Heaven is the love that remains after the loved one leaves. It's my grandmother's lilac bush and my mother's purple iris that bloom in my yard every year. It's your great-grandmother's drop-leaf cherry table and your grandfather's pocket watch. It's walking barefoot and wiggling your toes in the new spring grass.

It's juicy red strawberries and sweet drops of honeysuckle.

Heaven is all around us, but still we question its presence because we like proof and guarantees. This is our nature.

Maybe Heaven is life as we know it, minus the bad stuff. Maybe Heaven is discovering that there is no catch, and that we create all the bad stuff because we're complacent and ignorant and afraid to look at anything in a different light.

"What do you think Heaven is like?" I ask my 9-year-old niece.

"I think it's a place where the clouds are made of pink cotton candy and Old Yeller never dies," she says.

I would agree.

9. My Hometown

I rarely visit my old hometown, but circumstances took me down there last night and it was a sweet encounter.

I am with my husband, and we drive by my grandparent's farm on the edge of town where the huge maple tree has been replaced by a furniture store and I hiss and growl like a cat, clawing at the man who built this monstrosity where the old white farmhouse used to sit.

"Stop it with the hex stuff," my husband says. "Your grandfather would be proud of how much money the farm brought -- he would like knowing he was able to benefit his family in such a lucrative way and you know it."

Yes, I know it. Still I am comforted by the thought that the old pond still sits back in the woods – they didn't tear that away – and the thought that maybe the bullfrogs are still out there croaking at night, comforting some small child to sleep while her grandparents sleep soundly in the next room.

On down the road we pass the hardest part: It is the house I grew up in – the one in the middle of town with the big front porch with the old white swing and the big white columns and my mother's flowerboxes. It is impossible for me to look at this porch without seeing my mother stooped over her flowerboxes, pinching petunias.

Now a doctor owns the house and the flowerboxes sit empty. He has turned it into a business and I wonder just what it is that he does in our house, and I think how excited my mother would be at the thought of pap smears being performed in her kitchen.

Out front stands the huge dogwood that we used to hide in and scream at people as they passed by. Once my sister made me climb up in it and fall out, just as the lifeguard from the pool up the street drove by, hoping that he would stop and tend to my broken limbs. She knew exactly when he would drive by, and I fell out of the tree right on cue, but he did not stop. Such is the story of my life – the prince comes galloping to the rescue but takes one look at me and revs up the old white horse.

We get to the town square and I see my old friend's sister. It's been twenty-five years but she knows me and hugs me and this is good.

My husband is busy so I wander down the sidewalk and stare into the window of the shoe store that's been there since 1925. Suddenly I'm back in fourth grade with my best friends, picking out our new school shoes in September – penny loafers? Bee-bops? Around the corner stands the old Lay's five and dime and again I'm taken back. There's that pink and yellow flowered notebook from 1969 – the one every other girl in my class had at the start of the new school year.

And now I wander into the old corner drugstore – the one that still serves old-fashioned fountain drinks and the best vanilla shakes in the world. Walk in and you'll see big bottles of Watkins vanilla flavoring and a teenage girl in an apron behind the counter, and old men sitting at a table in the back.

I see a man I'd gone to church with, the old elder's son. "Do you remember me?" I ask.

"Why sure I remember you," he says, shaking my hand and smiling at me. "Why wouldn't I?"

My husband and I go to a restaurant and a classmate walks

by with his wife. He sticks out his hand and tells me his name without necessity. He was a senior when I was a sophomore, and one does not forget such things. His mother is also with him and a memory hits me: It is a slow hot day in July, and a friend and I have just finished grazing in her mama's kitchen – fried chicken, mashed potatoes, fresh green beans, fried corn, cornbread, plus other items too numerous to mention.

After lunch we become bored and decide to go out in the middle of the day and decorate various vehicles with shaving cream, our latest favorite pastime. We go over to this senior's house where his car sits out front and we squirt it with the cheap shaving cream in the red and white striped can from Fred's – four for a dollar. We circle his car, running and giggling until the cans are empty, then speed away happy. We go back to her house for dessert and the phone rings. It is the senior's mother. "You girls did a beautiful job," she says, "now get back over here and clean it up."

And so we do, and afterward we laugh long and hard and plan to do any future decorating at night.

Just down the road sits my old hometown with all its ghosts and memories. Sure, paradise has been paved by parking lots, but people still know my name and I am the luckiest of girls.

10. My Little Black Book

They say you can look inside a woman's purse and tell how she keeps house. Inside my purse you will find new and used toothpicks, shredded Kleenex, old grocery lists, gunky pennies, five tubes of lipstick, fifteen pens and pencils, half of a Pop Tart, pictures of my kids when they were young and cute, and my little black book.

My little black book says a lot about me. Inside the pages are names and addresses of those I have loved, liked, and lost. When a name becomes no more, due to death or dislike, I cross it out with a big X and jot down the reason. Most of the names are crossed out due to death, but some are crossed out due to dislike, disappointment, or dissatisfaction. Simply put, they are dissed from the pages of my life.

Next to Carl's X, for instance, I wrote "now in federal prison." Beside Bill and Sue, we have "divorced." Sandra, my cousin, has been crossed out ten times because she has a bad habit of moving. Same with all my nieces and nephews who are in college.

Some names are crossed out with no written reason, and only I know why the big X is there. I could have written "whiny," "annoying," "user," or "dog breath." For Helen, "hit a large nerve" would have sufficed. Instead, I wrote nothing and crossed her out twice.

So far, I've had an exciting life that has been filled with colorful people. My little black book reflects my journey, with all its twists and turns. Beside Dave's crossed-out name is the word "fartmeister." Now that's one X I don't regret. I had to wear a gas mask around the guy. Seriously. He could propel himself over to Afghanistan and send them crying deep into their caves forever.

But yesterday, I had a disturbing thought. Does God keep a little black book, and if so, does he use my methods?

Is my name crossed out in God's little black book?

Bill and Sue could have probably used a friend when they got that divorce. "Dog Breath" could have had a medical condition. And what role did I play in my fallout with Helen? Perhaps "Whiny" just needed to whine.

I've been thinking about getting a new little black book and including Carl, Bill, Sue, Dog Breath, Helen, and Whiny. Lord forgive me, I just can't handle Dave.

I gave up on Carl, Bill, Sue, Dog Breath, Helen and Whiny, and dissed them from my life. Will God dismiss me simply because I am not perfect?

I am told God doesn't give up on me, although I'm sure it's tempting.

There are lessons I have yet to learn.

I've always wondered how to gracefully bow out of an annoying relationship. Perhaps I'm supposed to stick around.

I've always wondered how to maintain a relationship with a twisted soul without allowing myself to become twisted. Maybe I just need to stand straight.

How does one separate the artist from the art or the dancer from the dance? I've always wondered. Perhaps they are one and the same. Perhaps it simply doesn't matter.

My new little black book is going to look different in ten years. Death will be the only reason anyone's name gets crossed out, and if I feel the urge to dismiss somebody, I will once again wonder about God's little black book.

I might even put Dave in there.

11. One of These Days

One of these days, I'm going to read all the books stacked up on my bedroom floor. I'm going to dust off my mantle and my piano and I'm going to sit down and write some new songs. I'm going to visit my 93-year-old Aunt Marguerite, and I might try to reconcile with a relative.

One of these days, I'm going to write one letter a month to each of my children, telling them about my feelings and perceptions at this stage of my life, so that they will someday have a written account of the changes they and their mother went through together – changes that will someday become significant to them.

One of these days, I will be a good grandmother like my grandmother was, but I am not in any hurry for this to happen. But then, lots of other people aren't, either, and they manage just fine. I'll bake fresh coconut cakes with my grandchildren, I'll sit on the swing with them out on my front porch, and we'll plant gardens together and grow old-fashioned flowers and bushes like wisteria, crape myrtle, sweet William, and peonies. I will read them poems from Robert Louis Stevenson's *A Child's Garden of Verses* and I will write letters to them, also.

I will take my grandchildren to church, but I will remind them that God still loves them even when they are bad, and that He always will, and nobody can ever take that away from them. I will tell them this early on, so that perhaps they won't spend much of a lifetime doubting this fact that some people call a notion. I will tell them that God loves them unconditionally, so that they won't waste time trying to prove the "Lowly Worm" theory true that is so prevalent in certain religions. Some of the lowliest worms I know attend church three times a week.

One of these days, I'll go to California and stare at the Pacific. I'll drive down Highway One in a convertible and I might even smoke a cigarette. I'll return home, thankful that a fantasy has been fulfilled, but I will find more satisfaction in knowing I stayed here through good times and bad, went to work most every day, struggled with PMS, teenagers, zits at forty and a difficulty accepting and integrating family dynamics that were embedded into my life.

One of these days, I'll arrange the pictures in my photo albums and look at the ones that used to be too painful, for I now try to look at the big picture and see both sides of the coin. I now know that while I did not paint the entire picture or design the coin, they are here to stay and it is my task to manage them creatively.

One of these days, I'll write a handwritten letter to an old friend, and I'll make a fresh blackberry cobbler like my grandmother used to make and give it to that relative that I have reconciled with. Maybe we'll sit down and eat it together, piled high with vanilla ice cream and disregard for calories, cholesterol and the past. Maybe we can look at the big picture and both sides of the coin together, and walk on in a path of acceptance.

One of these days, these things will happen. Perhaps I'll buy some fresh blackberries today.

12. Masterpieces

From my basement, I hear Pink Floyd drifting up from the computer and I smile because I know we've gone full circle. My kids can play "Comfortably Numb" full blast, because I like masterpieces. The fact that today's kids are listening to "Comfortably Numb," "Stairway to Heaven" and "Tangled up in Blue" tells me they recognize masterpieces themselves.

But masterpieces also encompass everyday experiences, such as snooping through your mother's Sunday purse for a piece of Juicy Fruit when you are a child, and hanging upside down from the dogwood tree in your front yard in July. Seeing the vastness of the ocean and smelling the salty breeze for the first time is a masterpiece, and so is a family.

A family is a work in progress, and the main artists are the parents, who, if they are smart, learn when to erase and change the colors and the brushes in search of balance and contrast. If necessary, they will rip up the portrait and burn it and start all over if need be, because smart parents know when something is terribly wrong with the picture. Generally speaking, if the picture looks perfect in the early days of family, it makes a great fire starter.

Things change. There was a time when reality terrified me, but now it is my greatest comfort. I am way past the early days of marriage when leaving and cleaving and becoming one were the ideal. Now I believe it's OK for our parents to want to spend time with their children minus their spouses, because it takes them back to their own sweet days of their early parenthood, and gives them a chance to reminisce. And while I believe the idea of becoming one has merit, I have found it impossible and unhealthy to completely meld with my husband, because we are different and that is OK.

After twenty-two years of marriage, he tells me he wants to sail around the world, and if he's going to sail around the world I can at least become a famous rock star. And though these possibilities are remote, dreams are the ultimate masterpiece.

When I compare our conversations of then and now, I see art. Consider this martial scene:

"What makes you think you look like a codger?" I ask.

"I looked in the mirror," he says.

"Well I'm getting old, too."

"Yeah but you don't look like a codger."

"That's because I wear makeup and dye my hair. Also my name means 'forever fun.' Yours means 'battleship warrior and sounder of trumpets,'" I say.

"But in the book of life, you ain't turned a page in fifty years," he says.

"That's because I'm only forty-five," I say.

The words my children say are pretty pictures, hanging in my mind. My youngest, whose diet consists of five foods, loves Kentucky Fried Chicken. A couple of years ago when I bought him a breast meal at the drive-through, he smiled and said, "Heaven is inside that box." The kid knows a masterpiece when he sees it.

Granny's journal was a masterpiece because she jotted down lines that were so sparse they somehow revealed much more. Oh, she never told much, and that is why her words were so powerful: *"September 3, 1963: Sister and Irene drove up and picked some turnip greens this afternoon." "July 20, 1976: I'm worried about Jane."*

My writing is wordier than Granny's, and if I switched to her minimalistic style my journal would look like this: *"November 3, 1992: The mopping did not go well." "March 17, 2005: Not a good day for a thong."*

Due to today's high-tech weather equipment, we are rarely surprised by snow. But today, on St. Patrick's Day, I woke up amazed to see the ground painted in white, a true masterpiece.

Don't wait to paint your masterpieces. Open your eyes wide and look around; look behind you, look ahead, and you will see them in full view.

13. Poolside Memories

School's out, the kids are home, and I close my eyes and drift back to summers past. Was it so long ago that I heard the screen door slamming shut and my mother screaming, "Either go in or stay out! If you slam that door one more time I'm going to lock you out for a whole week!"

In our town, we had three pools: the city pool, the aquatic-sized park pool and the country club pool. As a child, I spent much of my summer at the city pool up the street. There, I would sit with my friends at the bottom of the pool hosting "tea parties," and bumping rumps. For those who have never bumped rumps, it is simple: hold hands with your partner, hold your breath and go underwater, then put your feet together and you will automatically bump rumps.

At the city pool, we would eat large cookies from a Tom's cookie jar for a dime apiece – the kind with lemon icing on the top. These were the days before sunscreen, when the only suntan lotion was the Coppertone in the brown bottle – the one with the little girl whose swimsuit bottoms are being yanked down by the dog. With little effort, I can smell that Coppertone and taste the Fritos and the lemon cookies, and I can hear the squeals from jumping off the high dive for the first time.

During my teenage years, the happening place was the aquatic-sized pool or the country club pool. The summer of my fifteenth year, my best friend had long brown hair parted in the middle, and a tan to die for. I weighed as much at age five as my best friend did at age fifteen. That summer she wore a tiny brown and white polka-dot bikini, and the picture of her in the brown and white polka-dot bikini remains embedded in my brain as the ideal. Deep down, where irrational thoughts swim like minnows, I think to myself, "Someday I am going to look like that in a brown and white polka-dot bikini."

I miss the days of riding my bicycle home in the rain, and later being careful not to get the seat wet in the car after a full day at the swimming pool.

I recall the time the village creep flipped over backwards in his chair at the country club pool and his feet flew up in the air and we all laughed hysterically. There is a difference in the village idiot and the village creep: the village idiot was Noochie Booger and the village creep was a man who was once brilliant – a lawyer who had graduated from Harvard and had an unfortunate skiing accident which made him appear strange and perverted.

Women and children were afraid of him, and mothers warned their children to "Stay away from that man." That man, while in college, was on the diving team, and diving was the one skill the car accident did not steal from him. I loved to watch him dive and I loved to watch him walk, and once, just once, I wanted to see him approach a small child or a woman. He never did.

Now I regret laughing at him when he flipped backward in his chair, but such are the days of childhood. We must all forgive ourselves and be thankful, for we will one day be the victims of tragedy ourselves.

It's summertime and the kids are out of school. Already, they're slamming the screen door shut and I'm warning them to stay in or stay out. But I'm secretly thankful for the sound of the slamming door and all its memories. Think I'll go out and buy some Fritos and a bottle of brown Coppertone right now.

14. Hot Babes from Fly

Ilove the South, mainly because it is my home and I know nothing else. Even so, I can objectively recognize the unique advantages of Southern comfort.

Consider the Internet, for example. The down side to the Internet is the twisted filth, the vile sex that can be accessed at the touch of a finger. Luckily, the area in which we live will forever be a deterrent to this travesty. Who wants to see "Hot Babes from Fly," or "Bucksnort in Chains"? How about them "Sawdust Sex Pistols"? I am not by any means making fun of the Fly, Bucksnort, or Sawdust communities. It's just that the names do not lend themselves to sexual exploitation, and I'm glad. I love these places and their names, and I hope they are never swallowed up into larger, less identifiable towns and cities.

We're quaint, in our own special way. Where else but the South could you find the words *They called her Okra* engraved on a tombstone? And our respect for the deceased is incomparable. Since his demise, I've grown to love my deceased uncle, and the passage of time only makes my heart grow fonder. When my uncle died, not only did passengers pull over to the side of the road, they got out of their cars and sang the "Hallelujah Chorus." Such respect.

Southern language and Southern food are unique. Just the other night, my husband and I came home from a rotten, no-good, excuse of a movie. We could have eaten a three-month supply of turnip greens and purple hull peas for what we'd paid to watch that heap of Hollywood maggot food. When we got home, hubby sought comfort in a glass of cornbread and milk. He had his milk poured, and had his spoon ready to smash and stir. Salivating, he lifted the lid off the cornbread, but it was crustless.

"Who scalped the cornbread?" he cried out.

I flung him a Moon Pie (I keep them in my purse at all times) and he quickly recovered. I then made a mental note of the remark, "Who scalped the cornbread?" This line simply wouldn't be uttered anywhere else in the country, and I was touched by this poetic grouping of words.

First-year English teachers all over the South wring their hands in despair when their students respond with," I ain't got none."

"Where is your book?" they ask.

"I ain't got one," Billy says.

"And where are your pencils?"

"I ain't got none."

"Well, why doesn't your mother buy you some?"

"She ain't never home."

"And what about your father? Can't he buy you some pencils?"

"He ain't never home, neither."

"Have you ever heard of a double negative?"

"Yeah, I believe that's when two pictures is overexposed and stuck on the same piece of paper."

For the sake of their sanity, veteran English teachers in the South have accepted the fact that if parents say, "I ain't got none," their children will, too. Education doesn't amount to a hill of beans. If Southerners graduate from Harvard or Yale and move back to the hills of Snookeyville, their language will eventually revert back to their roots. Sure enough.

In a few more months, it'll be summertime in the South. I can't wait to grab a blanket, my husband, and a bottle of blackberry wine. We'll hop into his '58 Ford pickup, fly down that dusty road to the banks of Terrapin Creek, and watch the lightning bugs light up the Southern sky.

I can hear the catfish jumping now.

P⒜RT iv

Gimme That Old Time Religion

1. The Creature

(I) have always been blessed with people who exist merely to save my soul.

Many moons ago, when I was pregnant with my first child, a certain religious group knocked on my door and informed me there was no such thing as a burning Hell. According to them, a burning Hell was mentioned nowhere in the Bible. I was, however, requested to donate all my personal savings to their church and go door to door with them for the rest of my life.

I chose Hell.

The absence of a burning Hell was completely foreign to everything I'd ever been taught in church. I'd been trained to have the utmost respect for a burning Hell, because that was most likely where I would spend eternity, shoveling coal.

Several years later, when I was pregnant with my third child, I was planting onions in my garden when yet another ticket to Heaven presented itself. It was a gorgeous sunny day in April, full of promise and hope. The birds were harmonizing, the tulips were blooming, and the preacher was tapping his toes. Of all the nerve, he was standing in my garden with his arms crossed! I had visited his church, "the one and only true church," a few times, and had chosen to go elsewhere when my daughter kept referring to him as "the creature." She was a smart little thing.

I learned a long time ago that if you pretended everything was all right, people would leave you alone.

"I'm worried about you," said the creature, as he stuck an onion in the ground.

"Well, I'm doing just fine," I replied, flashing a smile and holding onto my belly. This was a great sympathy tactic upon which I relied during all my pregnancies.

The creature lingered and planted on. He was such a generous soul. I could tell he was thinking, "She's a little slow. How am I ever going to reach her? How can I sear her simple spirit?"

Little did he know I was playing dumb to get rid of him. I wanted to plant my own onions.

I kept planting and pulling an occasional weed. Suddenly, I came up with the perfect plan. Diversion was yet another tactic I had mastered.

I wiped my brow and looked concerned. "You know," I said thoughtfully, "I have tried and tried to get those neighbors over there to quit serving beer to their 14-year-old twin sons. On weekends and holidays, they sit out on their deck, fire up the keg, and offer fifty bucks to the fastest guzzler. Even their Chihuahua, Corona, gets plastered! Last week, he passed out and fell off the deck. After the contest ends, those next-door drunkards guide their wobbling teens to bed and then sneak back out to the deck to smoke some of that wacky weed they grow in their garden. See, there it is – hidden between the corn and the sunflowers."

The creature was mesmerized. He squinted and stepped toward their garden, his eyes oozing with opportunity. Meanwhile, I was smelling like a rose.

"If you'll excuse me," I said," I need to go lie down. "The baby is wedged in a knot."

"Of course, of course," the creature replied, as he stroked his chin and stared at the neighbors' garden. The salvation quotient was gaining every minute.

I never knew if the creature approached the neighbors or not. And the onions? Well, mine were crisp, succulent, and tasty. But the creature had planted his onions upside down.

Maybe I'll see them in Hell.

2. Sister Gloria

As a teenager, I was always baffled by the church experience. I never understood why, at church, my parents were nice to the preacher and the preacher's family that they made fun of outside the sacred walls.

I now know this is all part of the Southern tradition. I understand it, but still it makes no sense to me. There was one day, however, when the incongruence also got the best of my mother. One glorious day, my mother got mad and blew the preacher's wife straight out of the water.

Mama had her limits, and when she reached them, it was best to run.

It was the summer of 1976. I had an adorable wrap-around dress that my mother had made for me. It was light blue, and it showed off my sinful suntan.

One day in Sunday school class, my teacher, Sister Gloria, who was also the preacher's wife, was explaining the dos and don'ts of dating to the class of high school girls. It was unscriptural for a woman of "the church" to teach or pray in the presence of males after they had reached the "age of accountability," which was somewhere around the age of twelve. To me, this was the biggest joke of all about our church. *Age twelve?* Most males weren't accountable until they were dead. I knew that at the ripe old age of eighteen.

Sister Gloria would have made Mother Teresa look like a slut. She was thin as a rail and stiff as a board. She sat up straight,

128

with her hands clasped perfectly and her feet plastered together.

"Now girls," she said dreadingly, "do not hold hands with boys while you are alone with them." She leaned forward as if she were about to utter a great secret among women and whispered, "This gets their *wheels turning.*"

Gasps filled the air and Sister Gloria resumed her upright position and cleared her throat. The teenage girls all looked at each other gratefully. This tidbit of wisdom would remain with them for the rest of their lives.

"And," she continued, "dress modestly at all times."

I raised my hand. "Just what, exactly, is your definition of modesty?"

Sister Gloria looked at me in a most regretful way. It was the same way an employer looks at an employee right before handing over the pink slip. Sister Gloria squirmed and cleared her throat. She didn't really want to do this, but she had to. My soul was on the line.

"Well," she said flatly, "that *dress* you have on is immodest." She turned her head to the side as if she smelled a fajita fart. Then she regained her composure and cried out, *"I can see your slip!"*

Again, gasps filled the air.

I remained cool, but did not remove my eyes from Sister Gloria. I gave her the same penetrating stare that drove my mother crazy. Gloria squirmed and pleaded with her eyes.

"I see," I hissed.

After Sunday school, I told my mother what Sister Gloria had said. Suddenly, it no longer mattered that we were in church. Mama shot up out of her seat like a rocket.

It was still early, and preaching had not begun. People were still coming out of Sunday school, and during this time of transition it was acceptable to talk and socialize.

My mama marched right over to Sister Gloria and cornered her behind the back pew. *"I believe you have offended my daughter!"* she stated indignantly.

Sister Gloria nearly disintegrated. She opened her mouth to speak, but Mama did not stick around to listen. She marched right back to her seat and sat down assertively. It was highly impressive.

That evening after church, Sister Gloria and her preacher man came over to our house to apologize. They even gave me a key chain that said "to our special friend."

I later used the key chain to clean out my cat's ears. It worked better than Q-tips.

3. Funeral for a Friend

My sister and I recently attended the funeral of a home-town friend who was born into a family of men who have managed to convince themselves and others that they are the only people going to Heaven, because everyone else is WRONG.

Yes, the place was packed with uncles, brothers-in-law, cousins, espousing scripture and whispering about the will. They call themselves gospel preachers, but I prefer the term "sheep in black."

At many Southern funerals, a blanket of familiarity comforts those left behind. We go home and see all the old familiar faces and places, and manage to forget why we ever moved away in the first place.

But at this particular funeral, the blanket of familiarity was of no comfort. At every turn was a gospel preacher, standing guard like a gunman outside a Mexican bank, and I never even noticed the flowers because I was constantly on the lookout for my male captors; the preachers who knew me from my escaped past. They might call me the sheep in black but I prefer "the one that got away."

Now don't get me wrong. I am not referring to all preachers here, or even most preachers. I am referring to the ones who've managed to reach a smug, elitist pinnacle in life from which they look down and see entire oceans of black sheep, except when they look in the mirror. Luckily their numbers are few, because insanity will do that to a leader and his flock.

The casket was closed. The sons, handsome young men, watched their father lie in state with yellow tulips atop his chest.

I whispered to my sister, "I'll be right back if I ever get outta here," and went to the ladies room and thought about Mama. At funerals, she always said two things: "He looks so natural," and, "Death is such a final thing."

With the biggest of duhs, my sisters and I would march down the aisle with her and stare at the corpse, praying that just this once, she would keep her mouth shut.

The funeral began and my grief quickly turned to anger at the words that were both spoken and unspoken by the preachers. By the time they sang "Peace in the Valley," I was ready to belt someone, and I remembered why I left this town in the first place.

The dead cannot speak for themselves, and a funeral is not the place to point out deficiencies. Here, there were no highlights of a life well-lived, or memories of goodness and reassurance of grace. Instead, there were references to the term "gutter drunk," and mentions of judgment, eternity and HELL.

They sang "Softly and Tenderly," but the manipulation in the air interfered, and the words and the melody failed to stir my heart. The damage had been done, and I thought to myself, "Something is wrong with this picture. Only a heathen could botch 'Softly and Tenderly.'"

I almost went down there to speak up for our old friend. Who would have stopped me? Not only would it have fulfilled my dream of dressing up like Tina Turner and rocking down the sacred aisle, it would have set a precedent for women to speak up at Southern funerals. After all, we gave birth to these male pontificates. Verily.

I will miss my old friend. But I will take comfort in knowing that somewhere, there is peace in the valley and that he is there, at rest.

4. You Used to Have a Brain

When I saw them walking up my driveway and up my front porch steps I knew I should hide but my wheels started turning. The fun factor was simply irresistible to me so I opened the door.

"Hello," said the one on my left. "We're just sharing the word of Christ's Plan of Salvation – mind if we come in and have a chat with you?"

"I done been saved," I said.

"Oh, really?" said the one on the right. "And what is your branch of faith?"

"Heifers for Christ," I said. "It's a small group – made up only of women – but we got the Holy Cow in us, all right."

"And can you tell us just what it is that makes you believe in this church?" they asked.

"It's for women only; mainly large women who like to eat pig's feet and drink White Lightnin'," I said.

"But you don't look large," they said.

"Lately I been feastin' more on the white lightnin' than the pig's feet. Makes me feel a little closer to God somehow."

"Yes, but can you tell us exactly what it is that makes you believe in this church?"

"I done told you. Are you deaf or somethin'?"

"Why don't you just let us come in and talk to you?" We won't stay long."

"OK," I whispered, "but you'll have to keep your voices

down – my five husbands are down in their private pit, hand-stitching a quilt and roasting a buffalo."

And so the two young book-toting men came into my house and sat down on the couch, sitting straight as arrows, as if they had been injected with concrete.

"Want some coffee?" I asked. "Got a fresh pot of Folgers in the kitchen. Or how about some White Lightnin'?"

"No thanks," they said. "We want to discuss your spiritual future. Could you give us just a few more specifics on what it is that makes you believe in 'Heifers for Christ'?"

"Well, it's an old religion," I said, "founded by Wanda Woodcock over in Horsesnout back in 1832. Wanda was a smart old bird, and she wrote a book called *Heifers for Christ*. Back then women didn't have much of a voice and Wanda mysteriously disappeared. But her book lived on, and through the years a small exclusive group of women has carried on the tradition of her beliefs, which are based on grace, pig's feet and White Lightnin'."

"Well we totally agree that God's grace is fundamental to all salvation," they said. "But you must know that there is more to it than that. We are here to save you."

"I told you I done been saved," I said. "Now I think you better get goin' – I'm having a craving here."

"We'll only stay a little longer," they pleaded. "Here – would you like us to rake your leaves or wash your dishes or dust your furniture? We'll do anything you ask – can't you think of something?"

"Yes, I would like for you to lick my kitchen floor with your holy tongue."

They looked at each other with a "you go first" look on their faces.

"Well, what's it gonna be?" I asked. "Surely you know a tongue's made for more than talkin'."

"We will pray for you," said the one on the left, standing up. "That's about all we can do."

"That's all any of us can do," I said. "But prayer sure comes easier with a bolt of White Lightnin' and a pickled pig."

They left and I watched them walk down the street, robotically going from door to door, clutching their books and pressing on.

And as I watched them walk down the street I wondered just what it was that makes some of us more vulnerable than others and I thought sadly to myself, *"You used to have a brain. You used to have a brain."*

5. You Know Who You Are

Recently I ran into Betsy Lou, an old friend from my hometown. Betsy Lou and I have always been fascinated by certain religions practices that are unique to the South. Back in August of 1976, we parked outside a huge revival tent on the outskirts of town and watched and listened as people fell out in the floor and spoke gibberish. It was hard to tell if they were struck by the spirit or merely foolish.

Betsy Lou's teenage daughter inherited the gene of religious intrigue from her mother, and had recently attended a huge church revival with a friend. On the final night of the rousing, Betsy Lou herself slipped into back row of the gathering, standing room only. Once a zealot, always a zealot.

There were over a thousand people there, she said. At the end, the preacher pulled out a wad of paper and said, "I have in my hand a document from Amber, one of our devout teenage followers, containing the names of other teens who need to be saved. Amber has saved the souls of many, and has tried to save these, but still they turn their heads from God. You know who you are. Oh, ye lost souls who go down to the river at night and swim in the waters of lasciviousness, you know who you are. And though ye live in a land where the weed of the devil grows rampant, ye must not smoke it. You know who you are. Let not the bitter drops of alcohol wet your lips or parch your throat, even if you have been hauling hay all day for your uncle in the middle of August. Remember thy Creator in the days of thy youth, children, and walk the path of salvation, now. Tomorrow may be too late."

The preacher extended his arms and closed his eyes, swaying gently to the guilt of "Almost Persuaded." Slowly, then quickly, the aisles filled up with sinful teens. Betsy Lou put her hands over her eyes and peeped out, praying her daughter would not go forward, and she didn't. At least one sheep remained lost that night. Or did she?

"How does one know when she's saved?" I asked. "Do they get a receipt from God? Or a blank slip that says 'null and void'? And how, exactly, did Amber know those other teens were lost? And what gave her the authority to save them, anyway?"

"I don't know," said Betsy Lou, shaking her head in wonder. "This ain't what Brother Mayberry preached at all."

Betsy Lou and I grew up in a congregation that taught baptism was essential for salvation. Not just any old baptism, though. Complete immersion. My preacher even said that if your nose or your elbow were sticking out when you went under, you were lost and gone to cinder.

Behold! I happen to have tangible evidence that I am eligible for Heaven when I die. While rummaging through boxes many years ago, I found a Certificate of Baptism with my name on it, signed by Brother Mayberry himself. I wrote on it in bold letters, "Put this in my casket with me when I die," and stuck it in the vault with my will.

Above all else, I have sought truth in my life. And if I have learned anything at all, it is that God operates more out of love than fear, and that His grace is a real thing without a catch.

I no longer worry about the elbow or the nose or about whether or not Amber has saved any souls today. I do worry about the people who believe such notions, for they are missing the point and wasting precious time, one of God's greatest gifts.

You know who you are.

6. Church Signs

Southern towns are laced with church signs and ours is no exception. Recently I spotted this admonition on the sign outside a local church: *"Don't wait for the hearse to take you to church."*

Is this supposed to be **INSPIRING?** Come on, people, we can do better than this. For example:

~ Jesus loves you but that's about it

~ Bring your children up in the nurture and admonition of the Lord and they will move to California

~ For remember, the very hairs of your head have roots and you need a highlight

~ Hell's hotter than a hog pen in July

~ Pray without preaching

~ Why people are unwilling to admit they are wrong: **BECAUSE THEY BELIEVE THEY ARE RIGHT**

My favorite church sign is down on Interstate 65, somewhere close to Birmingham: *Go to church or the Devil will get you.*

Mind you, I think church signs have merit and I attend church regularly myself. But I believe God has a sense of humor, and I also know that church isn't the only place to find God.

Maybe I'm wrong, but I suspect God grows weary of clichés and pontification. I believe he welcomes new twists on old themes as well as the average reader. New and improved signs such as these might just allow Him to sit back and breathe a little easier:

~ A catfish a day keeps the Devil away

~ His eye is on the sparrow 'cause he's tired of watching you

~ Because you're vile, I walk the aisle

~ Pride cometh before a cavity search

Most of us fear Hell and have perceptions of fire and brimstone and a grinning Devil with a wagging tail, holding a pitchfork and getting ready to spear it straight through our hearts. But wait, there's more! Hell is a place where the river runs dry and the tulips are black as a crow. And Hell's connotation varies according to one's nature and profession. Hell for English teachers is no red pens and double negatives scrawled all over the wall, a pit where the milkshakes boil and the beer's run dry and you're always craving a cigarette but they ain't got none.

When I was a child, I spake as a child and I still do. I used to ask, "Where is Hell, Mama?"

"Well hon I don't know," she'd say. "Just leave me alone for a little while and we'll talk about it later."

Five minutes later I'd go back into the kitchen and ask, "Mama, you never did tell me where Hell was. Where is it? If it's down in the ground how do you get there? Is there a big slide or somethin' like they have out at the park? Does the Devil really have a pitchfork and horns? Do you think I'll go to Hell, Mama? Will I? Will I?"

"Well hon, just leave me alone for a little while and we'll talk about it later. *As the World Turns* is almost off and then you can go to the store with me. I need you to run in and get me some L&Ms, and if the preacher sees you tell him they're for your daddy."

139

But Daddy's in *England,* Mama! And if I lie I'll go to Hell! Do you think I'm going to Hell, Mama? Do you?"

"Well hon, good night -- if you don't leave me alone I believe I will go insane. Why don't you run out and play in your sandbox for a little while. Or go read *Little Black Sambo.* You love that book."

That settled it. If Mama wasn't worried about Hell, then I wasn't going to worry about it either. I went to my sandbox and later read *Little Black Sambo* and later still went with Mama to Star Market to buy her some L&Ms because I was bolder than she was, and I still am.

Now my own children ask me where Hell is and I tell them it's right here on God's green earth, in the heart of an addict and the soul of a liar. Hell lies in the absence of our belief in God's grace, His greatest gift of all.

Now why couldn't Mama have said that?

7. Church Chat

It is significant that in the church in which I grew up, I always sat on the left wing. Although at the time I was not familiar with left-wing politics or right-wing politics or any politics at all, I'm surprised my church even had a left wing, due to the ultra conservative nature of the church leaders, who were all male. They got to lead the singing and lead the prayers and pontificate about scriptural versus unscriptural topics such as kitchens in the church building and the possession of church buses and instrumental music, for we were to sing and make melody in our hearts as the Bible so clearly stated.

Although I no longer attend this church, I have come to appreciate my experiences there because I am intrigued by bizarre and ludicrous events in which seemingly intelligent people participate.

It was a family affair in my church, one where my parents and grandparents and aunts and uncles and cousins attended, and aside from the bizarre and ludicrous events it provided a sense of hometown security for which I am thankful. The people there have known me all my life, and that's a comfort.

But now I know that as I sat there in the pew on the left wing, it doesn't get any more right wing than that. In fact, the right wing had broken off and was drifting through outer space, toward a black hole where we were beckoned to get sucked in at all times.

Being a rebel at heart and always one to question things, I

was both an embarrassment to my family and a pain in the butt to the elders and preacher. In church, I fantasized about dressing up like Tina Turner in a micro mini skirt, grabbing the microphone and strutting my stuff down the aisle while belting out "Proud Mary" with Jimi Hendrix accompanying me on guitar and Janis Joplin singing background music.

I knew that in order to preserve any semblance of sanity, it was necessary to tune the preacher out at all costs, so while he screamed and stomped and banged his fists on the podium, I read the Bible. Often when he would cite scripture I would look up the same verse and derive a totally different meaning from "Love thy neighbor" or "Sing and make melody in your hearts." Where in the Bible did it state that I was not to sing "Proud Mary" in a mini skirt with the aid of Jimi and Janis?

Back then I was a smoker and the verse "pray without ceasing" intrigued me. I'll bet when Jesus wrote that one, he was going through nicotine withdrawal.

I did get to talk in Sunday School, and I asked lots of questions, such as, "If buses and kitchens are unscriptural, then how are we to provide transportation and food for the hungry and needy? If instrumental music is unscriptural then why is it OK for the song leader to use a pitch pipe in church? And aren't those flowers unscriptural – where in the Bible does it say to decorate the pulpit with flowers? And for that matter, these songbooks will probably send us to Hell because they were not sanctioned by the Holy Word and some of the songs were written by Methodists and Baptists and other heathens."

The men were never able to answer my questions but they did give me lots of killer looks.

Of course, dancing and drinking were sins but since we

were told there was no degree of sin I chose these two as my favorites and on Saturday nights I would party with friends while hanging off the left wing with my seatbelt unbuckled.

Grace was a joke, literally. The preacher would say, "Oh, our Methodist friends down the street are good people but they're going to Hell because they believe they're saved by grace. Hah!"

I always wondered how the preacher could bear for his "friends" to go to Hell, for if I believed my friends were going to Hell I would be sad.

But I am older and wiser now and recognize that many elitist groups obtain a false sense of security by convincing themselves they are the only ones who are right. This tendency is not unique to my childhood church and it is not unique to religion, but it is indeed insane.

I no longer fret over triviality and I am comforted by the words that I so often heard sung in my church: Jesus loves me this I know, for the Bible tells me so.

That's plenty for me.

8. Our Father Who Art in School

Forwarded e-mail tends to repeat itself, and I am amazed at the seemingly intelligent people who send messages full of propaganda. Yesterday I received four e-mails regarding prayer in schools, urgently coaxing me to forward the message to everyone in my address book so that prayer could be reinstated in our public schools. As an added bonus, I would receive a free Old Navy gift card.

I'd like to know when the freedom to pray was removed. How is it possible to prevent someone from praying?

I frequently volunteer in a public school, and I see prayer. Kids pray to pass the test. Teachers pray for three o'clock. Principals pray for conferences in Gatlinburg.

Our poor children, I am told, are forbidden to pray in schools. And it is this absence of prayer in schools that has caused everything from school shootings to pinworms.

Back when we had prayer in schools, the grass was always green, the sky was always blue, and the sun was always shining.

Back when we had prayer in schools, classrooms were devoid of profanity, teachers felt safe, and Bayer aspirin was the only drug around. Were these trends absent because of public school prayer, or were they absent because parents disciplined their children at home? Back then, more parents were actually at home to manage their family lives.

It is crucial that we understand the cause and effect aspects of then and now.

Some people would even suggest that back when we had prayer in schools, folks from different political and religious walks of life held hands and sang "Row, Row, Row Your Boat" on a daily basis.

And then they had to go mess up a good thing.

"It was the strangest thing," says Louise, an 85-year-old geometry teacher at the high school. "The day they banned prayer in schools, a big pink wart popped out on my left elbow. Had a little smiley face right in the middle of it."

"My little Billy had never had a cavity until prayer was banned in school," says Martha Joyce. "A month later his front teeth rotted out and he later went into a full set of dentures by age seventeen."

By golly, let's just mosey on back to the good old days. Let's reinstate school prayer in public schools.

Picture this with one eye shut:

Prayer is reinstated and Ms. Chalkdust, the first-grade teacher is kneeling before her class on her polar bear prayer rug. "Dear Lord," she says, "thank you for acknowledging my prayers. Thank you for allowing me to live in a country where I can live an openly gay lifestyle. Thank you for allowing me to preach as an ordained minister in my church. Thank you for allowing me to be pro-choice in my beliefs as a woman. Thank you for giving me the opportunity to influence these young minds in prayer and in accordance with your divine love and acceptance."

In walks Mr. Newsocks, the principal. He interrupts Ms. Chalkdust and says, "Whoa, there, Nelly. You wait just wait a minute, sister. You're not supposed to be leading a prayer. Why, you're a woman! And what's this 'openly gay lifestyle' hogwash? You can't be carrying on like that around here.

It's blasphemous!"

"Why Mr. Newsocks, where have you been for the past thirty years? You can't discriminate against me on the basis of my sexual orientation or my religious beliefs! These children have a right to be exposed to free thinking and free religion! Don't you realize that's one of the benefits of the reinstatement of public prayer? Isn't this what you wanted? After all, you were the biggest advocate in the county for school prayer. Be careful what you wish for, Mr. Newsocks. Be very careful."

Prayer still runs rampant in our public schools, and it will as long as people want it to. Oh, the words may not be fancy and loud, and they may not be read from an index card, but God still hears them.

I'm told He prefers silent prayers anyway.

P(A)RT v

The Facts on
Holidays and Seasons

1. Summer Vacation Journal

May 18: Last day of school. Kids ran out screaming while I clung to their teachers. Hard to let go – why does it have to be like this? School could last all year! Brought kids home. Quickly consumed three-liter Coke, large bag of Doritos, lemon icebox pie and five bananas. An hour later asked, "What's for lunch?"

May 19: Crashed into garage door while singing along to "Smoke on the Water." I'm into a lot more than Deep Purple here. Four hundred fifty six bucks, to be exact. Hubby doesn't know yet. Cooked him Cherries Jubilee for dessert and later gave him European massage.

May 20: Dishwasher clogged up and icemaker froze up. Hubby spotted the garage door. Saw him cry for the third time in eighteen years.

May 21: Computer modem tore up, VCR died, shower leaked into basement, and electricity got cut off. Forgot to pay light bill last month. Oops!

May 22: Garbage disposal severely clogged with potato peelings. Hubby cried again. Industrial strength Mr. Plumber finally pulled through for us. I love him.

May 23: Cleaned out fridge and found a ham in my crisper. Kids had water balloon fight in the kitchen while I mopped the floor. Innovative win-win situation.

May 24: Garbage disposal clogged up with water balloons. Mr. Plumber doesn't do rubber. Hubby had to fish out plumber snake apparatus and crawl under sink. Pipe broke and showered him with coffee grounds and animal fat. Cried again.

May 25: Forty degrees outside. Global warming is freezing my buns off. Marigolds are rigid and petunias are shivering.

May 26: Heating element in dryer burned out last Tuesday. Hung towels on clothesline and forgot about them for three days. Towels were rinsed with fresh rainwater from heavy downpours. Hubby thought this was great. Felt like a real prairie woman.

May 27: Had PMS. Choked the ice cream man for playing "Pop Goes the Weasel" at suppertime.

May 28: Still had PMS. Grabbed super soaker and blasted cat out of zinnias at 7:00 A.M. My flowerbed is not a litter box.

May 29: Stepped on a giant hairball at two in the morning. Soaked my feet in Epson Salts and stayed up to watch an old Elvis movie. Ate large supply of cashews. That cat is going to be sorry.

May 30: Felt adventurous. Painted my toenails and pinched my petunias.

May 31: Simmered white beans and turnip greens on the stove all day. Kids scattered in all directions so I was home alone. Tomorrow it's sardines.

June 1: Took kids to the pool. Painted smiley face in my belly button but wore purple one-piece. Felt happy just knowing it was there.

June 2: Took kids roller-skating. Fulfilled latent desires to be roller derby queen.

June 3: 103 degrees outside. Got down on my knees and thanked God for the air conditioner.

June 4: Air conditioner went out.

June 5: Air conditioner still out. Hubby and I took an ice bath together. Not sexy.

June 6: Good news: cold air. Bad news: big bucks.

June 7: Bought hubby new box of hankies. Now cries on daily basis.

2. Halloween Buster

Back in my childhood days, Halloween was a night in which kids would throw a sheet over their heads, cut eyes in it, and run out the door with a brown paper bag from H.G. Hill that would be filled to the brim with candy by the end of the night. There was no talk of tainted apples or poison candy, and there was certainly no talk of Halloween being a day to worship the Devil.

Back then, things were simpler and grown-ups had more to do than to sit around and twiddle their thumbs, wondering what holiday they could mess up next. Today it seems we have too many grown-ups who have time to sit around and ponder the Satanic origin of things, such as holidays.

I am not one of those grown-ups. Halloween is my favorite holiday and it always has been and always will be. For years I have dressed up as a clown on Halloween and passed out candy to the trick-or-treaters, but I'm tired of the clown thing. The polka dots are faded and the hat is torn and I hate that stupid nose. I've changed. This year, I've ordered a French Maid costume from Frederick's of Hollywood, complete with 6-inch spike heels and fishnet stockings, and I plan to surprise my husband dressed in this garb with a bucket of Almond Joys and Sugar Babies, his favorite. I'll do the tricks and he'll get the treats and I might just get a new red convertible Volkswagen Bug out of the whole deal.

Of course, I'll probably wear the clown suit while passing

154

out the candy to the trick-or-treaters, or I might be a vampire. That way I could leave on the black eye makeup when I slip into my French Maid costume later in the evening. Just take out the fangs and I'll be set to go.

And another thing, the local animal shelter has put a ban on the adoption of black and white cats, which is fine by me. But why doesn't the kitty cult go after the deviant Siamese? Every year for the past six years I have put a sign around my Siamese cat's neck that says "Maim me, I'm yours," yet no one has taken her. It's not fair. This year I'm going to crown her with a set of devil horns and see if I have any luck.

Also, the Ghost Walk that is planned for Saturday night at Rose Hill Cemetery has been mainly praised, but also criticized as disrespect to the deceased who are buried there. Lord willing, I will be at that Ghost Walk, taking the tour and listening to the stories and paying my respects to those gone before me. I like to think that when I'm dead and gone, people will think enough of me to saunter across the grounds of my resting place and remember me with tales and stories. Ghosts deserve a little attention, too.

Today we live in a world in which people have a need to be critical, a place in which people have enough time on their hands to sit around and conjure up whiny thoughts and deeds. It's too bad these people can't get a life and enjoy it like the rest of us.

You ever know if this Halloween may be your last. And for that reason, I plan to max out in my French Maid costume and live it up while I've got the chance. Could mean a drive across Highway One, overlooking the Pacific in my new red convertible Volkswagen Bug. We'll see.

3. Holiday Stew

alloween will be here in almost two months and it's a good thing because there is a Ninja Turtle shell underneath a table beside the piano that has been there since last Halloween. I was unaware of the hard plastic shell until I spotted it in the middle of the couch the other day.

"What's this Ninja Turtle shell doing on the couch?" I asked my husband.

"It's been under the table beside the piano since last Halloween," he said.

"Along with the Santa Claus hat, the baboon mask and the blow-up Easter bunny."

"You're kidding!" I said. "Where is all this stuff and why haven't I seen it?"

"It's inside the big black cauldron underneath the table beside the piano. I figured it was your holiday stew."

I could have sworn I put all that stuff back in the attic. Oh well. What difference does it make anyhow? It's not like somebody suffered bodily harm because of this holiday oversight.

The whole thing got me to thinking about Halloween, my fave holiday.

"Do you realize Halloween will be here in two months?" I asked my husband.

"What do you think I should be this year?"

"You could go for the eclectic Godzilla look and wear the Ninja Turtle shell with the baboon mask, your reptilian gloves and your clown hat," he said with a hint of silent resignation.

When my husband married me, he thought I was normal and I thought that I had potential. I was wrong and he was, well, surprised by my sense of adventure and lack of housekeeping skills. Still, he has never been bored and there is something to be said for that.

I used to feel a tad guilty for being a Betty Crocker factory reject and a Girl Scout mutant. But it was precisely that sense of adventure that made me what I am today and helped me to overcome my housekeeping guilt.

When I die, I do not want the words "She was a lovely clone" inscribed on my tombstone. In fact, I do not want a tombstone at all. I want a plastic urn placed on top of my mantel.

Seriously, I have given this some thought. The urn will need to be plastic so that it will not break when the new wife dusts. Also, if there is a new wife before the respectful period of one year, my children have agreed to place a few of my ashes in the new wife's pepper shaker.

Some people may find this strange, but to me it is a comfort to think that wherever my family goes, I will go also, placed in a safe warm haven above the fireplace.

It's been a long year and a hot summer and I'm ready for things to cool down. I'm ready to bring up my glass pumpkin jar from the basement and fill it with candy corn. I want to sip hot apple cider and wrap up in a blanket at the high school football games. I want a harvest moon, a hayride and the first fire in the fireplace.

Long as I'm not perched on top of the mantel.

4. Inflatable Santa

They say confession is good for the soul so here goes: I have a strong desire to shoot all the inflatable Santas in town. I particularly would love to go Rambo on the inflatable Winnie the Poo and the inflatable Tweety Bird just down the road, and when I see them lying crinkled and flat on their backs on a cold winter's morn, it makes me happy.

So there.

I was talking to a fellow columnist yesterday, and I asked, "What are you doing?"

"I'm writing my column," he said. "What are you writing about this week?"

"Promise you won't steal my idea?" I asked.

"I promise," he said.

"I am going to write about how I would love to shoot all the inflatable Santas in town."

"Awwwwww, don't do that," he said. "That's cruel."

"Don't go goody-two-shoes on me here," I said. "You know in your heart you feel the same way."

Although he never admitted to such a thing, I knew I was right, and I hung up knowing he wished he had thought of it first.

Now don't get me wrong, because I do not own a gun and I have never even shot a gun. I would never actually act on the urge to shoot the inflatable Santas. Still, when I drive by the inflatable Winnie the Poo and the inflatable Tweety Bird, I feel like a man on the first day of deer season. Furthermore, let it be here and forevermore known that it is our business what we choose to place in our yards, be it yard gnomes, inflatable Santas, pink flamingoes or commodes with petunias.

When my children were young, I would have probably bought the inflatable Santas myself, for I know that young children adore them. But my children are older now, and one of the benefits of being the parent of an older child is the right to fantasize about shooting inflatable Santas and elves. Surely I have earned this much.

Folks, the inflatable market has just begun and inflatable stock might just be a wise investment. Before it's over we will have inflatable politicians, inflatable trees, inflatable furniture and even inflatable houses. We will even have inflatable cats and dogs, and there will be a huge decline in the kitty litter market. With each passing second, researchers are working furiously to solve the problem of "deflation by cold" among the inflatables. If no solution is found, we can all move to Florida and live by the inflatable beach.

Now that my soul has been cleansed, I am going to take a walk around the block and look at the withered Winnie the Poo and the crumpled Tweety Bird.

Ah, Christmas. Let us savor each moment.

5. Summertime

We are deep in the throes of summer. The heat, the humidity, the slamming doors of kids running in and out of the house, squirting each other with water guns and sitting like vampires in front of the computer, fixedly staring at Diablo II and Starcraft Expansion Set.

It's been a weird summer, somehow. Everyone I know, including myself, is hot, bored, weary and slow. Some summers are like that, I suppose. Or maybe we're just getting old. For one thing, summer is the great transition. Kids get out of school and are in need of a plan, and mothers wrack their brains trying to devise that plan. And for those of us who fail to come up with a plan, our children end up sitting in front of the computer like vampires, fixedly staring at Diablo II or Starcraft Expansion Set.

Summertime has special meaning to me because it is when I get my mammogram. Much has been written about the mammogram, because it is an experience unique to women that men cannot begin to grasp or appreciate. As I was walking out the door for my mammogram last week, I said to the kids, "I'm leaving now."

"Where are you going?" my 14-year-old son asked.

"I have to have a medical procedure done."

"What is it?"

"Have you ever heard of a mammogram?"

"No."

160

"Do you know what boobs are?"

"Yes."

"When you get a mammogram, you get your boobs mashed flat in a machine, and then they take pictures of them."

"Are you serious? Is that why they start to sink as you get older?"

Ah, the sinking ship of Mammogram. I can hear it now on the faint horizon of the future: "I'll always remember the good ship *Mammogram*. She was a real floater in her day, but all good ships must eventually sink."

Summertime can also mean the preparation of children leaving for college for the first time. My daughter leaves in one month, and I'm getting nervous. Why does so much of life consist of holding on and letting go at the same time? I look outside my den window at the empty spot where a wooden swing set used to sit. Yes, there are ghosts out there in my backyard. I can see her swinging high in the air, hair flying and feet bare. I watch her take off on her bicycle without training wheels for the first time. I see her running through the rainbow of the waterhose, with her brothers and sister and neighborhood friends.

When I close my eyes, I can hear the laughter and the squeals, but when I open them, it's quiet out there. The grass is still and the trees are big and tall, a tangible reminder that in life, we do change and grow.

Oh, I don't mean to whine, because even this summer has had its moments. Back in June, we went to the beach and the weather was great, the food was tasty and I read two books. One night, we went to a small amusement park where my husband and I rode a Ferris wheel that overlooked the ocean, complete with full moon. When we got to the top, he put his arm around me and kissed me, and I thought of a Joni Mitchell song called "Both Sides Now," that spoke of moons and Junes and Ferris Wheels, and looking at both sides of love and life.

I strive to look at love and life that way, too, Joni. And I hope I always will.

6. Snow Songs

Far as I'm concerned, Bill Hall was the only weatherman who actually knew anything about the weather. I have not even watched the weather since Bill Hall left, I miss him so. Among other things, he invented Snowbird, who is still around and is a nostalgic reminder of the great weatherman himself.

One reason I liked Bill Hall was because he did not taunt us with huge, feathery flakes of snow. He did not threaten us with bowling-ball-sized hail or tsunamis in Bucksnort. When Bill Hall told us it was going to rain, it rained. When he said it was going to snow, it snowed. And when it quit snowing in Middle Tennessee, he retired. Who could blame him? I'd like to be catching catfish on the banks of Terrapin Creek and raising pole beans and silver queen corn and okra myself.

We are approaching the end of January, once again snowless. All we can do is sit around and reminisce about the old days when it snowed back in the sixties. I remember the snow of New Year's Eve 1963 when we got eighteen inches and my family and four other families got stranded in one house, all twenty of us. I still have the picture of my parents' light blue Volkswagen, parked in a snowdrift with snow up to the windows. I can still smell the cozy breakfast aroma of bacon and sausage and pancakes and coffee that my parents' best friends prepared for all their guests at the Stranded Inn.

Yes, these snowless days are depressing. My friends and

I long for the good old days, at least the friends who are old enough to remember. Lately, to ease our longing, we have been writing snow parodies while sipping hot buttered rum around the fire, and this helps. Given enough rum we can convince ourselves that a magical snowfall has blanketed our town. In time, Frosty himself is standing out in the back yard in a Speedo, arms outstretched with a pipe clinched between his coals of teeth.

My favorite parody is "Snow Dancing, " sung to the tune of "Slow Dancing."

Snow dancing, swaying to the music
Snow dancing, just me and my, my, my, my bird,
Snow dancing, swaying to the music,
Channel 2 man didn't say a word

And then there's the song my son wrote for his girlfriend upon leaving her parents' house at the hour we used to refer to as "the shotgun hour," when the girl's father makes his point without saying a word. His sonnet is titled "I'll Be Back Before the First Snowflake Falls," sung to Freddy Fender's "I'll Be Back Before the Next Teardrop Falls."

If it brings you happiness
I will let you get some rest
It's supposed to snow tomorrow, after all
Mama's done bought milk and bread
To make sure that we're all fed
But I'll be back before the first snowflake falls

No, I don't watch the weather since Bill Hall left, but I do occasionally take a peek at the Channel 4 website, whereupon I recently discovered that not only can you obtain the weather forecast, but also the "mooncast," which is poetic as Robert Frost himself. Yesterday's mooncast said, "Today's moon is crescent and waxing." Just out of curiosity, I clicked on another local website to read their mooncast: "Today's moon has a big hairy barnacle that's going to barf out hail." Lies, all lies.

Thanks to Bill Hall, I'll always be a Channel 4 woman.

7. Thou Shalt Not Speak in This Manner

It all happened very fast. I don't know why it happened, it just did. Maybe it was the Christmas holiday season. Maybe it was my fundamentalist upbringing, I don't know. All I know is at five o'clock on a recent Tuesday afternoon, a distinct Biblical dialect began to emerge from my mouth. I was driving up to The Mall at Green Hills with my daughter, who had recently completed her first semester away at college.

"I have to have some new clothes, Mom! And all my new friends drive BMWs, so I'm hoping I'll get one for Christmas. Or even one of those little Volkswagen Jettas would be nice. Oh! Did I tell you? I'm going to study in Paris next spring!"

I slammed on the brakes at Harding Place and hit a possum. "Why dost thou tell me these things?" I screamed.

"What is wrong with you?" she said. "And do you realize you spread possum juice all over the road? That's environmentally unclean, you know. They don't even have possums in my new town."

"Thou shalt not boast or commit gluttony," I said.

"And thou shalt not add to or take away from the Ten Commandments. I've been an arrogant glutton for the last four months and you've never cared. Why start now?"

"Thy father and I can no longer afford gluttony. We have chosen sloth."

"Sloth? You can't do sloth! Who's going to pay for my

college? Who's going to send me to Paris? Have you considered adultery?"

"Thou canst pay thine own way to Paris. Henry County is not that far away."

"Why don't you let me drive, Mother? We are very close to a mental hospital, and I'll drop you off while I go to the mall. Do you have your credit card?"

"I beseech ye not to speak to me in this manner. I am thy mother and I am sane and serene."

"But you're a sloth! What am I supposed to do now? Why couldn't you have chosen greed, or pride? Anything but sloth!"

"I hath already practiced greed and pride, and both faltered in pain. Slothfulness is smooth and easy ... possibly the greatest of sins."

"What is this? Seven deadly sin week?"

"Why do the heathen rage?" I asked.

"OK, Mother, that's enough Bible jargon. Time to get back to your normal wacko self. This is even worse."

"Speak to me softly, or a beast with seven heads will devour you."

"But I thought Dad was playing golf in Phoenix."

"Thou ungrateful child! And dost thou still resist prayer? Thou art told to pray without ceasing!"

"OK, Mom – you win. Lord, bless the Harding Place possum that it may not get run over again ... that it may be scooped up before the maggots arrive ... that all its other possum friends are saved."

"Thou shalt not get sacrilegious with me, child!"

"Why not? Maybe you need to sit inside a whale and forget about life for a while."

"Do not speak of Jonah in this manner!"

"OK, how about this one: Ashes to ashes, dust to dust, all I want is a bigger bust!"

And so it came to pass, that we returned to our homeland and all talk of gluttony, plagues, leprosy, and flirting with the Devil disappeared.

By Christmas day, I was back to normal, stuffing myself with turkey, dressing, sweet potatoes and spiral ham.

"It's good to have you back, Mom," my daughter said, "and I love my new Jetta! But aren't you eating just a little too much? You don't want to ruin your June Cleaver figure, now do you?"

Indeed, gluttony is difficult to overcome at Christmastime.

8. Lilacs and Petunias

I just couldn't help it. There he was sitting all alone, so I went over and sat down beside him on the floor and crossed my legs, Indian-style. The mall was deserted and the Christmas gnomes were standing still and the dancing bear was plugged in tight to the battery recharger, and suddenly I was alone with Santa, in a fluff of red and green.

"Ho! Ho! Ho! "he said. "And what do YOU want for Christmas?"

"You can't give me the things I want," I said, "but still I yearn for them," I said.

"Try me," said Santa. "You might be surprised."

"I want my mama, I want a new song from Johnny Mercer and Billie Holiday, and I'd like to write an old-timey song … something like 'And Now I Think of You.' I'm in a real time warp here, Santa. "

"Go on," he said, lighting his pipe and kicking off his black boots. His bare feet were firm and tan and his toenails were nicely groomed. Young feet.

"I thought you were supposed to be old and fat and jolly," I said, "but here you've got nice tanned toes and a good pedicure."

"This ain't about me," he said. "It's about you. What else is on your mind?"

I sat and stared straight ahead at the eight reindeer and the three-foot candy canes stuck in the floor, wondering what was holding them up, and suddenly I had the urge to open up to

Santa and tell him things I couldn't even say to myself.

"I feel.like last year's boots and yesterday's paper," I said, "and at night I dream of earthworms and bulls. Also, there's this stupid line that keeps running through my head – *Lord I cried when Dumbo died.* And lately I've been thinking they should start making Pepto Bismol in different colors, like neon green or horse-hair brown."

"Go on," said Santa, with his head thrown back, staring at the roof of his portable gazebo.

"Things drive me crazy," I said. "Things like ice-chomping, lip-smacking, apple- crunching and mispronunciation of words. I work with a man who says 'dramastic' all the time, and he thinks it's really a word. And it terrifies me that not one of our presidents has ever been able to pronounce 'nuclear.' Also, I despise acrylic sweaters, plastic geese and Tide commercials."

"Anything else?" said Santa.

"Yeah, there's another woman I work with – a religious zealot, always passing out 'Journey with Jesus' brochures and angels and crosses and such. The thing is, she's been married five times and thinks she's holding the one ticket to Heaven. She's always been on a crusade for Christ, but when it comes to getting lonely, Jesus sits on the back burner with the stove turned off."

"I see," said Santa, exhaling with a smile. "Is there anything you like?"

"Yeah," I said. "I like old friends and old pianos, warm oatmeal cookies, tulips and Hank Williams songs. I like eating pancakes in the middle of the night, skinny dipping, soft summer rain, blackberry cobbler, fried okra, white teeth, pink lips, massages, Jacuzzis, big juicy steaks, and old red bicycles. And then there's *The Wizard of Oz*, Beethoven, lilacs and petunias.

170

I like a good cry, playing in the sand with my kids and walking along the beach with my husband at night in July."

Santa wiggled his attractive toes and sat up. "Go home now," he said. "Curl up on the couch and watch *Dumbo* and have yourself a good cry. Kiss your children goodnight and snuggle up with your husband before you drift off to sleep, for tonight you may dream of lilacs and petunias."

"No more earthworms and bulls?" I asked.

"Time will tell," said Santa. "After all, it's only a dream. You've got some pretty good realities here – cling to them while you can."

Lilacs and petunias? I can sleep on that.

9. The Dreaded Christmas Letter Redux

ow that Thanksgiving is behind us and the Christmas season has officially begun, I'd like to send a reminder to those who feel inclined to boast about details of their children's potty training accomplishments, cum laude status, ski trips to Aspen, and that fabulous bonus Richard received for his brilliance and sheer perfection. And please, if you stroll topless along the French Riviera, don't send pictures.

The best part about Christmas is the cards sent from friends, relatives, and acquaintances, old and new. I always find it refreshing to read the personal little notes these folks have jotted and scratched onto the paper.

The Christmas *letter* is a different story altogether, sent mainly by pompous souls who think their recipients actually give a flip about their numerous accomplishments. I have one thing to say to these people: *WHO CARES?*

The same people always send the dreaded Christmas letters, year after year. I can picture them now, strategically plotting and planning next years' chain of events.

For the last sixteen years, I have received a Christmas letter from Amy, beloved mother of Bobby and Tim. I can tell you when Bobby and Tim took their first step, when they caught their first fish, when they made the basketball team, and when they got their first girlfriend. However, I cannot tell you anything about the time Bobby got drunk and obliterated the car, or the time Amy flew off to Maui with a rich codger from California, because Amy always omits these minor imperfections.

You see, the writer of the annual Christmas letter is a suffering idealist who struggles to believe all the hogwash she writes, and therefore wants to suck us into her belief system for validation. In her twisted mind, a part of her believes that if she actually writes this stuff down and mails it out to 500 people, it must be true.

A cousin of mine always uses the annual Christmas letter to proclaim her godliness to the world. Now that I think about it, this is perhaps the essence of the annual Christmas letter. This cousin, however, is more blatant than most. I don't actually receive a Christmas letter from her, because she has given up on me, but my sister does. Every year, Sis calls and reads it to me over the phone while we take a stroll down Barfomania Lane and squeal with laughter.

This cousin, who is now a "shamelessly silly grandparent," is queen of the annual Christmas letter. Now that she has turned all corners of the facade and is perched regally on the pinnacle of pretense, she can kiss the wart on my foot.

If I'd written a Christmas letter in 2003, it would have gone like this:

> *Dear Friends and Underlings,*
>
> *What an eventful year! Back in May, I rolled off the couch and onto the floor, where I proceeded to crawl over to the TV and turn off Guiding Light for good. After all these years, I decided it was time to give it up. Then I stood up, dusted off my gray sweats, and took a walk around the block! I became so inspired that I returned home, sat down at the computer, and began to write my*

memoirs. Both of them.

After twenty years of marriage, Carl got a little fidgety and took up golf. Don't you just love those little white balls? I now know all about putters and drivers and bogeys and such. As always, our talents and interests complement each other so well. When he leaves, I drink cappuccino and work on my 300 page "to-do" list," and it all works out perfectly.

Daisy, our eldest, still prefers thugs to "nice boys," but we are hoping she will outgrow this phase of her life. Carl is afraid the thugs will steal his golf equipment, and so am I. Iris, our second child, began to emit some frightful adolescent utterances back in October, but has since calmed down. Could have been the Halloween influence. Teens are faced with so much these days.

Blade, our son, has grown into such a handsome young lad. Oh, he still blows his nose on an invisible Kleenex and he still runs into a tree every now and then, but such is life.

May the year 2004 bring you everything you want, and the strength to cope with everything you don't want.

Happy holidays,
The Rose C. Glasses Family

Maybe Christmas letters aren't such a bad idea after all.

10. My Blue Jay

I t's spring. The daffodils and tulips are blooming, the birds are building their nests, and the mules are back in town for the annual Mule Day festivities.

A pair of blue jays have been building a nest outside my window. Every morning when my husband and I sit on the couch and drink coffee, I watch, eye level with the bare branches of the maple tree. The male blue jay, the one with the brighter blue chest, diligently flies up to the nest with twigs, sticks, and pieces of paper. "I admire that about him," I say to my husband. "Just look how much care he's putting into the nest. Where do you think his wife is?"

"She's probably out shopping for little birdie clothes," he says. "Or she could be out with the girls, or getting a massage or a pedicure."

"Well, she'd better enjoy life while she can because soon he'll fly the coop and she'll be feeding four hungry mouths. Is it possible he'll stick around?"

"Some birds are monogamous," he says, and somehow I know this is the case with my blue jay.

Every morning I sit and watch as he hops around from the tree to the deck, surveying the territory, carrying a new twig to the nest to put on the finishing touches. I think he is the superman of all blue jays, and I can even discern his chirp from all the other birds outside.

Yesterday he swooped down and grabbed a berry, and in

an instant he was back in the nest, ever on the lookout for his precious wife who makes an appearance every hour or so.

"Just look at him," I said to my husband. "He is so devoted to her. Do you think it is possible that I have bonded with that bird?"

My husband looked at me. "With you anything's possible," he said. And then he burst out laughing like it was funny.

Late yesterday afternoon, my husband was out on the deck grilling pork chops, and my blue jay sat perched on a branch, watching him. I burst out the door and said, "There's my blue jay," and he flew off.

"Have you ever tried the subtle approach?" my husband asked. "You might be amazed at how effective it is." Again he laughed as if he had said something funny. And then he said, "You really should stop bestowing human traits onto animals. It's unhealthy."

"If I bestowed human traits onto my bird," I said, "he'd have a TV, a remote and a port-o-potty up there by his nest."

The whole thing has made me wonder. Where do birds go when it rains, or when they get cold? Do they mourn when their nest blows out of the tree and their eggs are eaten by cats? And are they really monogamous?

I think they are. In my heart of hearts, I think my blue jay stood up on his two hind feet, stuck out his big blue chest and sang "I Honestly Love You" before asking his bird to marry him. And knowing him as I have gotten to know him these past few days, I'll bet he even slipped a tiny ring made out of clover onto her left foot.

It could happen. If birds can fly, surely they can love.

P(A)RT vi

Goulash

1. My Chimney Sweep

The Christmas season came and went, and we enjoyed the usual traditions, with the exception of the cozy fire-in-the-fireplace scenes. Oh, we tried all right. We bought the wood and we opened the damper and lit her up. Problem was, the smoke went in the house rather than up the chimney.

"What will Santa Claus do?" I asked my husband. "We can't expose him to all this soot!"

He just stood there and stared at me with that "Will you always be like this"? look on his face.

And being a man who believes that things fix themselves, he said, "Don't worry. I heard the fire marshal say that if you keep a big roaring fire in the fireplace every day, it cleans out the chimney all by itself, creosote and all."

In years past, the chimney has indeed stopped smoking and started drawing on its own, but not this year. Every attempt to light a cozy fire and snuggle up on the couch resulted in opening doors and windows and turning on fans in 20-degree weather.

"So what do you want to do now?" my husband asked me one night.

"Well now that we've barbequed the children, I guess we could go to a movie," I said. "Or perhaps we could call a chimney sweep."

"A chimney sweep?" he cried. "Why do we need a chimney sweep? After a couple more fires, everything will be just fine. You'll see."

Two days later, things were still smoking, and the only thing good about it was that my husband was wrong.

"I'll look in the yellow pages and call a chimney sweep," I said. "You just go back to work and I'll take care of it."

I had never called a chimney sweep before, and because of the Mary Poppins influence, I was a tad excited about talking to one. I looked in the yellow pages and saw only two listings, so of course I called the one with the larger ad. To my surprise, a woman answered the phone, and I explained our dilemma to her.

"What?" she screamed. "Do you mean to tell me you have lived in your house for twelve years and have never had your chimney cleaned? Why, you're lucky you haven't burned down the whole neighborhood! Besides that, we're booked and can't see you till the last week in January."

I wanted to scream, "Oh, go feed the birds!" and slam the phone down, but I was at her mercy. "Do you know any other chimney sweeps I could call?" I asked in a meek voice.

"Yes, I do know of one," she said. "Be sure to tell him I recommended him."

And so I called the second chimney sweep, and once again his wife answered the phone and listened to our dilemma, minus the lecture. She even said he would be over in two days!

Sure enough, the chimney sweep and his assistant arrived right on time, and cleaned out our chimney in less than an hour. The assistant stayed up on the roof, but the chimney sweep stayed in the house, whereupon I took the opportunity to ask him a few questions.

"I've never met a chimney sweep before," I said. "Do you get a lot of references to Mary Poppins and 'Feed the Birds,' and all that?"

"Oh yeah," he said, laughing. "But it's all a lot of fun." There was a twinkle in his eye and a smudge of soot on his nose, and with his assistant up on the roof, I wondered if together, they might be Santa Claus.

When he finished the job, I was sitting on my hearth and he got down on one knee and handed me his card. "I am your chimney sweep," he said, "and I always want to be your chimney sweep. If anything ever happens to your fireplace or your chimney, I want to be your chimney sweep forever."

I just thought that was the cutest thing I ever heard, and I immediately said yes. In my mind, I envisioned future bullies coming up to me, and I would spew, "Back off or I'm gonna call my chimney sweep!"

Thanks to our chimney sweep, we now have cozy fires in the fireplace without opening the doors and turning on the fans. Now if that's not a true Mary Poppins moment, I don't know what is.

2. Southern Resume

I t's the start of a whole new year, that glorious time of resolution and change. Many of us are seeking a job change, so here are some resume tips, designed in particular for the Southern woman.

If you want a good job, quit rinsing those turnip greens and work up that resume. You have to have a resume, and remember, "resume" doesn't rhyme with "assume."

Before you unveil your newly polished resume, check out these resume rules for Southern women below:

~ Beauty before Brains: A little cleavage brushed with gold-flecked powder can downplay typos quicker than a possum goes splat. And twirling a dandelion between your thumb and index (pointer) finger sends a timeless subliminal message.

~ Understatement is good. Fatten up for the kill and downplay your Southern credentials in the job interview. Forget about "yes, sir" and "no, sir." This is the time to sit proud and tall, sling your hair back and act like a cube of confident ice. And no matter how tempting, don't write "Mammy's sawmill gravy" as one of your greatest accomplishments.

~ It's OK to fudge. If you have never had a job, conduct a private séance and invite Barbara Walters to inhabit your body for fifteen minutes. Recent research indicates séances work just as well on the living as the dead.

~ If you have fifteen kids at home, tell the head honcho you're barren, just like Holly Hunter in *Raising Arizona.*
~ Leave Bubba at home with the kids.
~ No mention of white beans, shotguns, or homemade sausage.
~ If you are seeking a job in a field in which you have no prior experience, by all means, lie. Southerners catch on real quick, and your new boss will never suspect a thing.
~ Leave your chewing gum on the bedpost, honey.
~ Avoid use of double negatives. Examples: "I ain't got none," "He ain't got none," "I didn't get none'," and "He ain't never gonna get none."

Below are two examples of a job interview; one proper and one improper.

PROPER:
Employer: Do you have any experience in this field?
Southern woman: Why yes, I have ten years of experience. I was general manager in my last job, and received a rave recommendation from my boss when I left.
Employer: Why did you leave?
Southern woman: I felt a calling to work for the Peace Corps in Ethiopia.
Employer: And did you actually do this?
Lying Southern woman: Yes, and it was the most fulfilling experience of my life.

IMPROPER:
Employer: Do you have any experience in this field?

Southern woman (smacking her gum and twirling her hair): Naw. But I ain't stupid or nothin'. I learn real quick.

Employer: Have you ever had a job before?

Southern woman: Yeah, I worked at a drive-thru car wash/catfish place. My boss begged me to stay.

Employer: So why did you leave?

Southern woman: I had to miss 'Days.' But it was sort of fun, wearing high heels and Daisy Dukes, holding a sponge in one hand and a catfish in the other.

So there you have it. Follow these guidelines and you'll have a job quicker than you can say "Avon calling."

3. Life's Embarrassing Moments

We've all had them – moments when we've wished we could disappear, or go back in time to erase the words we uttered.

I recall the day they called me from school to come and pick up my kindergartner. Head lice were running rampant in his classroom, and it seemed his head was the Alpha host. On the way home, we stopped at the grocery store to pick up some head lice shampoo. We were in the dairy section, beside the eggs, when he said, "Now what kind of eggs do I have in my head, Mama? Will they get this big?"

I leaned over and whispered, *"Be quiet."*

"But I don't want to be quiet!" he said. "I've got eggs in my head!" Tears started streaming, and a crowd gathered, his Sunday school teacher among them. My child screamed and kicked. "I've got eggs in my head, I've got eggs in my head, and they're going to hatch!" Some little old lady handed him a Kleenex and a Tootsie Roll Pop. He flung it at her and bonked her in the head.

"Why, you little imbecile!" she said.

I hope she got eggs in her head.

Our cleaning lady happened to be standing over by the cheese. When I rolled by her, she leaned over and whispered, "I ain't cleaning up after no head lice, no sir-eee. I don't want no eggs in my head!"

My child clawed at his head hysterically. "I've got eggs in my head!" he kept screaming, over, and over, and over.

The store manager pranced over to my cart, wearing rubber gloves and a fake smile. "Lady, perhaps you should slip out the back door. Your son is very upset. Forget about paying for your groceries, and take this complimentary case of head lice supplies." He leaned closer and confidentially whispered in my ear, "You're going to have to declare war on the little suckers. If you don't, he'll have eggs in his head for a long, long time."

He was right. Head lice are a force to be reckoned with. I ended up shaving my son's head and spraying it with Jungle Gardenia. Hey, it worked.

And then there was the company Christmas party, back in 2005. We were at a swanky hotel in Nashville, where the women were all cloned up and the men wore tuxedoes.

I was standing among a circle of women, beside my colleague Betty, when I spotted a creature grabbing olives off of dirty plates and popping them into his mouth like popcorn. He was even tossing them up in the air and catching them between his teeth. He looked like a Southern Godzilla. Ugliest man I ever saw.

"Who is that man?" I asked. "He looks like Godzilla. Can you imagine curling up to that scaly thing every night?"

A hush fell over the circle, and Betty's nostrils flared. Suddenly she looked like Godzilla, too. "Yes, I can," she said. "He's my husband."

"Oh," I said. There was nothing else to say. At that moment, I vowed never to speak again. After that, I dyed my hair, moved to another town, and complimented everyone, no matter how undesirable I thought they were.

Ironically, my most recent embarrassing moment occurred at

the same grocery store in which the head lice incident took place.

I was over in the produce section, sampling grapes and cherries. My grandmother always did this, and she was a fine person.

I moved over to the vegetable section, next to a male employee who was misting the cauliflower. He looked a bit like Johnny Depp.

"Mind if I sample your zucchini?" I asked.

He grinned. Nice teeth.

"Sure," he said. "Name the time and place."

I give up.

4. Southern Writers Conference

(M)any proclaimed writers don't actually write; they just hang out at writer's conferences and buy books about writing. While I actually do write a lot, I'll admit I attend writer's conferences for all the wrong reasons. The truth is, the conversations at these gatherings intrigue me, particularly within the confines of a social setting, or a "meet and greet."

Recently I had the chance of a lifetime to attend a writer's conference especially for Southern writers. It wasn't that other regions of the country were unwelcome; it's simply that they wouldn't want to be there. Writers from other parts of the country don't hear violin music when they talk about possums, moon pies, turnip greens and Bud Light commercials.

Imagine my delight when I found myself alone in a corner with the author of *How Much Beer Can I Drink and Still Lose Weight?* Not only is this book humorous, it is going to be the best selling diet book of all times. And just when I thought it couldn't get any better, I met the author of *I Know Why Mee-Maw Pooted When She Walked Across the Room.* Watch the bookshelves for this one, due this September.

Another highlight of the conference was meeting the Betty Blake, author of *Top Five Lists and Knockout Comebacks.* Here is an excerpt from her book:

Top Five Lines You Will Never Hear Your Man Say:

1. Here, Babe ... let me massage that bunion.
2. Hon, would you bring me the feather duster?
3. Just a sec, gotta grab my lip plumper.
4. Your birthday's coming up ... diamonds or rubies?
5. You look tired... lie down for an hour while I whip
   up a little chicken cordon bleu.

And Betty Blake's number one comeback for e-mail "Christian" mortgage lenders:

1. Can you tell me about your Leviticus special?

In a similar vein, I met the author of *For the Over-Forty Insomniac Crowd: Games to Play with Your Spouse in the Middle of the Night.* Suggestions included the following creative ideas:

1. Name that Bone
2. Counting the Shadows from the Mini Blind Slats
   on the Ceiling
3. Toe Wars
4. Old Orifices
5. This is the Way We Brush Our Teeth

Yes, it was an exhilarating, fun-filled event, but the highlight of my weekend was meeting the authors of *Running Naked in the Snow: A Guide for Menopausal Women,* and *But I Thought Mr. Ed was Real : How to Put on Your Big Girl Panties and Clomp Through Life with Success.*

I only squirmed once through the entire weekend, when the

author of *How Much Beer Can I Drink and Still Lose Weight?* caught me off guard and asked, "So when are you going to submit your book?"

"I have to find it first," I said.

"Find it?" he asked. "What do you mean? Didn't you spend ten years writing it? Doesn't that mean anything to you?"

"I think it's under my bed," I mumbled. "You know how we writers like to sabotage ourselves."

Luckily, the author of *How to Put on Your Big Girl Panties and Clomp Through Life with Success* rescued me just in time, and right then and there I silently vowed to put on my big girl panties and crawl under my bed and find that manuscript and submit it.

I'm not holding my breath, but we'll see what happens.

5. Regret

For all sad words of tongue and pen, the saddest are these, "It might have been."

—John Greenleaf Whittier, poet (1807-1892)

L ast Monday night, a sunset of orange, lavender and pink blanketed our town like I'd never seen before. The sharpness of the orange horizon mixed with pastels of lavender and pink made me feel like a moving subject in a painted landscape. I happened to be at the right place at the right time, right in the middle of the stroke of the brush.

It reminded me of a Bible verse about how the sun shines on the rich and the poor. As I drove through the back streets of town, this sunset made even the rotted wood on dilapidated houses seem new. In the midst of skinny cats, rusted-out cars, the courthouse and the Polk Home, the sunset was out there for all to see, like a great equalizer. Still, I remembered that underneath that sunset blanket lived a town full of people whose hearts were both breaking over loss and bursting with joy, for life unfolds in its own time.

And now, back in the kitchen of my real world, the plates sit still in the sink ... the cat sleeps still in the dining room chair, and I just sit and think about concepts like stillness and waiting and regret.

Out in town, I hear truck drivers' engines roar down the highway ... they've been up all night, driving and thinking about what might have been … arriving at a quiet resolution around 4:00 A.M.

If I'm here in fifty years, I'll wish I'd been kinder to that cat in the dining room chair. I won't regret my cluttered sink or my messy dining room table, but I may regret the stillness of my piano that waited for me to sit down and play a C chord, then an A minor, my favorite.

If I'm still around in fifty years, I hope I can't ask myself this question: "Where have I been all my life?" I hope I will have made the most of my life, for who can escape the shape of a life?

In fifty years, I'll remember that sunset of orange and pink and lavender, and how, at just the right time, it fell upon a cozy town that I belonged to. A town with a house for me to go home to, with a husband and kids, a couple of cats and a warm bed.

And I'll be glad I wrote it all down … glad I had the where-withal to catch up with life from time to time.

That's plenty for me.

6. Dear Abby

ove over, Dear Abby! It's my turn to write an advice
column:

Dear Anonymous Mother,
I am all alone in this world. My parents died ten years ago
and I recently killed my ferret with a bowling ball. Sometimes
I get so lonely I send "thinking about you" cards to myself.
Any advice?
 Signed,
Gutter Girl

Dear Gutter Girl,
Stuff the ferret and don't forget your birthday.
🐭 🐭 🐭 🐭 🐭

Dear Anonymous Mother,
I am a huge advocate of the death penalty and I have a
great idea. Don't you think it would be good if they beheaded
the criminals after execution, and mounted their heads on the
prison walls like deer? Also, I think prison guards and other
prison personnel should wear shirts that say "You book 'em –
we cook 'em."
Will you support me in my worthy cause? I'll even send you
a free shirt!
Signed,
Fry Daddy

Dear Fry Daddy,
Be sure to send me a picture of yourself, too. I want to be
able to recognize your head up there on that wall.
ʊ̃ ʊ̃ ʊ̃ ʊ̃ ʊ̃

Dear Anonymous Mother,
I am a 48-year-old real estate agent and don't know where else to turn. This is a highly personal matter, and it recently cost me a huge sale. I just can't tell my doctor.

I believe I am too old for tampons. Last Tuesday, I was showing a million-dollar antebellum mansion. The prospective buyers and I were standing on the veranda when I suddenly sneezed.

To my horror, my tampon blew out, flew over Mr. Southern Plantation's head, and hung in the magnolia tree like a Christmas ornament.

What should I do?
Signed,
Sneezy

Dear Sneezy,
Have a hysterectomy or try to get on the Jerry Springer show.
ʊ̃ ʊ̃ ʊ̃ ʊ̃ ʊ̃

Dear Anonymous Mother,
I am a 68-year old woman who has always itched to be a rock star. All my life I've cooked, cleaned, and ironed, and I'm sick of it. And I don't like my grandchildren, either.

Please help. I've got a Tina Turner trapped inside the bustle in my hedge path.
Signed,
Private Dancer

Dear Private Dancer,
Rock on, Granny! Climb that stairway to Heaven! Just wear
your earplugs and look out for Ike.

ಠ ಠ ಠ ಠ ಠ

Dear Anonymous Mother,

I am writing to you for reassurance. I don't really have a problem. The thing is, I love to go to the dump. I get an adrenaline
rush from the moment I climb into the truck until the moment I
see the recycling bins. I especially like seeing the old cracked
lamps and the plastic dressers. Once I saw a live rat and couldn't
sleep for days. Would you like to go to the dump with me?

Signed,

Trashy

Dear Trashy,
Hell, no.

ಠ ಠ ಠ ಠ ಠ

Dear Anonymous Mother,

I write to you from Sweden, where I recently became a
woman. Question: Do you think I could be President of the
United States?

It's something I've always wanted to do.

Signed,

Estrogenia

Dear Estrogenia,
I don't see why not. This country is always in need of a
woman president and a great scandal.

ಠ ಠ ಠ ಠ ಠ

Dear Anonymous Mother,

Do you believe in reincarnation? I'm convinced the sparrow who perches herself on my deck every morning at 5:00 A.M. is actually my dear Aunt Sally. How can I know for sure?

Signed,

Birdbrain

Dear Birdbrain,

Ask her.

ॐ ॐ ॐ ॐ ॐ

Dear Anonymous Mother,

My husband sometimes dresses up like Tarzan and beats his chest when he wants to have sex. It used to be an occasional thing, but it's been a week since he changed out of his leopard-skin loin cloth. Also, he has installed a swinging vine from our bedroom ceiling. Help!

Signed,

Me Tired Jane

Dear Jane,

Grab Cheetah and get away from this lunatic. Spiderman is much more exciting, and he's out there somewhere, just waiting for you.

ॐ ॐ ॐ ॐ ॐ

Dear Anonymous Mother,

Thousands of starving Ethiopians will die if you don't forward this message on to 500 people. It's your choice.

Signed,

Lover of guilt-ridden chain letters

Dear Lover,

I'm sending you a one-way ticket to Ethiopia so that you can go over there and feed them yourself. You caring soul, you.

ॐ ॐ ॐ ॐ ॐ

7. Van Gogh's Ear

Yet another difference between women and men: Men will cut off a body part to prove a point. Everybody knows that Van Gogh cut off his ear and later painted his famous *Self-Portrait with Bandaged Ear.* As a child, I loved to look at Van Gogh's self portrait with the bandaged ear, and my mother was also intrigued. She'd say, "Wonder why he'd do such a thing – I heard his girlfriend dared him to do it and he did to win her love."

In truth, Van Gogh cut off his ear over an altercation with Paul Gauguin, then wrapped it in cloth and went to his favorite brothel and presented the ear to a prostitute.

In a less manly fashion, Geraldo Rivera has recently stated that he will shave off his mustache if Michael Jackson is found guilty of child molestation.

The big baby. What's so great about Geraldo's major appendages that he can't spare one of them? He could auction off an ear on eBay and contribute the money to the war in Iraq or the tsunami relief fund. But no, he's going to shave off his Brillo Pad mustache in an attempt to prove yet another ridiculous point, his specialty.

If Geraldo Rivera's a journalist, then I'm a neuroscientist. He's the arrogant king of sensationalism, doing anything that will draw attention to his measly self. In a show on plastic surgery, Rivera once had fat sucked from his buttocks and injected into his forehead in a procedure to reduce wrinkles, and that is precisely what is wrong with Geraldo: his butt is in his head.

In contrast, Van Gogh's memory lives on. He was a brilliant artist who painted many masterpieces and inspired other spin-off businesses that exist today. Van Gogh's Ear Café in Union, NJ, is "an eclectic and unique coffee lounge and restaurant." In addition, Van Gogh's Ear is an immensely popular band in the United Kingdom with a strong local following in their home county of Cambridgeshire. In Guelph, Ontario, you can visit a popular nightclub called Van Gogh's Ear and listen to a variety of music.

And while these businesses are capitalizing on the mystique of Van Gogh's ear story, I think Van Gogh would understand and possibly approve, for if he understood anything at all he understood human nature and highlighted it on canvas. If anyone ever opened up a restaurant called "Geraldo's Mustache," the place would be shut down for cockroaches.

Now that Geraldo has threatened to shave off his mustache if Michael Jackson is found guilty of child molestation, the jurors will no doubt re-think any inclination to prosecute in light of such travesty, for the world simply cannot go on without Geraldo's mustache.

Perhaps in the end, Jackson will be declared innocent and Geraldo can accompany him to Neverland. By day, the two of them can ride round and round onthe carousel, hanging offin childlike glee, and by night they can eat popcorn and watch movies and jump up and down on the bed together to their hearts' content, until the end of time.

8. The Roll

I'm at that age where you can't remember phone numbers, and when you finally do, you can't dial them without your reading glasses. And so it was, that while I was driving down the road yesterday, I dialed the same wrong number for the second time in a week. Much to my delight, on the other end I had captured a local drunken Dave Chappelle in the midst of his Lil' Jon routine.

"Hellooooooooo?" he says.

"Oh I'm sorry," I say. "I've got the wrong number."

"WHAT?"

"I'm sorry, I've got the wrong number."

"Okaaaaaaaaaaaaaaay."

I'll admit, I'm a sucker for Chappelle's Lil' Jon routine. So suddenly I hear myself asking, "Who is this?"

"Well who is *this?*" he asks in a perky slur. I remind myself this is the second time I have gotten this particular wrong number with the drunken voice of Chappelle's Lil' Jon. It has to be fate.

"You have an interesting voice," I say, laughing.

"Well you got a weird voice, too!" he says.

"Now wait a minute -- I didn't say you had a weird voice, I said you had an *interesting* voice."

"Well haaaaaaaaaaaaaaay!" he says. "Would you like to come over and git to know me a little bit better?"

"Oh, no," I say. "I couldn't do that. I've already bothered you enough with the wrong number. I promise I won't do it again."

"Well that's okaaaaaaaaaaaaaaaay," he says. "Talk to ya later."

I could have just hung up the phone when I got the wrong number, but something stopped me. I have always been this way, much to my mother's horror.

Back when I was just a child, we were eating out at the local diner after church on Sunday. The fact that I can remember the story is proof that I was way too big for a high chair, but I was the baby in the family and the high chair also kept me confined.

Mama must have been tired that Sunday, and failed to notice when I was rocking around in my high chair and toppled over and crawled out. Before she could stop me, I had wandered over to a man from church, an elder, and asked him if I could have his roll.

"Why certainly you can have my roll!" he said, and proceeded to give it to me. By the time I got back to my family's table, I had the entire roll stuffed in my mouth and I felt happy, as if I had just caught a big fat blue gill or discovered a dollar bill on the sidewalk. As I chewed my roll, my mother was mortified but I was in the midst of church people and I was safe.

While they watched, Mama hissed behind her June Cleaver smile, "What in the *world* is the matter with you? You know better than to go up to a man and ask him for his roll!"

It was the last time I sat in a high chair, and I no longer ask people for their rolls. But if they offer, I usually say yes. My mother and I were different like that. But if I didn't possess such personality traits, I would have missed out on talking to the drunken Chappelle while he was smack dab in the middle of a buzz. I would have missed that big warm roll and the horrified look on my mother's face, and if I hadn't been so bold I might still be stuck in a high chair today.

Sometimes you just have to seize the moment. That roll sure was good.

9. Conflict Enhancement

 don't believe in conflict resolution. I believe in conflict enhancement.

Take Deb, for instance. Take her far, far away.

Deb is the most annoying acquaintance I have ever known. She is a spoiled, controlling, whiny know-it-all who gets on my last nerve. I have worked with her for ten years.

I've tried to ignore her. I've tried to avoid her. I've nearly gone blind, trying to see the good in her.

I've turned my left cheek. I've turned my right cheek. Now I'm turning both cheeks.

Bottom line is, I don't like her and she doesn't like me. We both acknowledge and accept this, and have consequently made great strides in our relationship. It's all very adult and mature.

"Deb," I say, with my feet propped up on my desk and my hands clasped behind my head, "the very sound of your voice makes me want to shoot ducks. You're such a brown-noser. Who do you think you're fooling?"

Deb cackles and pops a blueberry into her mouth. "Your shoes are disgusting," she says. "Where did you get them? Family Dollar? You wear the tackiest clothes I have ever seen. You could at least polish your toenails."

Together we chuckle. "Do you remember the time you tried to take all the credit for the Bilcon account?" I ask. "The one I landed? I hated you so much that day. I still hate you, but I feel so much better about it now. Everything's all right, because now

I accept you for who you are, you lousy, no-good, rotten, whiny, transparent, gravy-sucking wad of fly flim. This is great."

"Isn't it, though?" Deb says, as she sits up straight with much enthusiasm. "Do you remember the time you misspelled 'occur' at the Valentre presentation? I was promoted the very next day. You didn't even know how to pronounce 'conglomerate.' I just love stupid people, especially you."

My eyes grow misty with reminiscence. "You are the most two-faced person I've ever met," I say to her with great respect. "You should give lessons. Do you remember the time I told Candice you said she was fat? We ganged up on you and watched you cry and lie like the dog you are."

"And do you remember," Deb says, "the first time I accused you of sitting on your butt one too many times? It was your turn to wash the coffeepot, you lazy fleabag. There was mold growing in the lid. Of course, you probably considered that a delicacy."

We laugh long and hard, then look at each other somewhat uncomfortably. There is a hint of vulnerability in the air.

"Are you feeling what I'm feeling?" I ask. "I think I'm beginning to *like* you! Do you want to go get a cup of coffee?"

Deb hesitates, and twirls her hair. "Are you kidding?" she laughs. "I wouldn't be caught dead with you. What if I ran into one of my sorority sisters? I'd get kicked out!"

"Whew!" I say. "That's a relief. For a minute there, I could have sworn you were my best friend."

If I'm your best friend, you'd better be running for cover," says Deb. "And while you're at it, buy yourself a new outfit, and get rid of that perm. The eighties are dead."

It's Friday afternoon, and we get ready to leave. I turn out the lights, and Deb locks the door. We walk down the long corridor together, where she always turns left and I always turn right.

"Goodbye, Deb," I say. "And thank you for being my nemesis." "Anytime," she says. "Anytime."

10. Cyber Party

What did we do before e-mail? Was it only a few short years ago that we had to pick up a phone or a pen to keep in touch?

My e-mail address book contains fifty addresses. In addition, I am familiar with people's names that appear on e-mail I receive from my top ten e-pals.

I've never met Uncle Herb, but I sense that he is unreconciled. His e-mail alternates between nasty blonde jokes, vulgar drunk jokes, and messages of divine inspiration. You never know if he's going to send *Deep Throat* or *The Sermon on the Mount.*

And then there's Martha, clone of Ms. Cheap. Last week she wrote, "Yet another sock idea! Last night, I snipped the toes out of my husband's nylon sock, and made a coat for Virgil, our ferret. Virgie loves it, and he looks adorable! See attached picture."

Cousin Sue just recently got online, and does not realize her messages are dated. Not only does she believe her messages are brilliant and fresh, she believes people love to receive them.

Cousin Sue is the queen of e-mail prayer threat chain letters. "Forward this prayer to everyone in your address book," she writes, "or you will die from gluttony within the hour."

I wonder what it would be like to throw a party for my extended cyber family. How would it be to come face-to-face with Uncle Herb? Does he look like John the Baptist or Hugh Heffner? And does Martha actually wear a wrap-around skirt made from the Sunday comics?

I imagine the party would go something like this:

"Oh, Sue," says Martha, "I just loved that five-page testimony you sent about the little girl who was scooped up by a pelican and flown across the Isle of Capri! You were the 45th person to send me that story, and I printed them all out and made myself a new jumper, using only scissors and Elmer's glue. Isn't it adorable?"

"Heh, heh, heh," says Uncle Herb, chewing on a cigar. "Do you know what Elmer's glue is really made of?"

Over in the corner is my pal Sally, author of *How to Tell if Your Kid's a Dumbass*. She's talking to Phil, author of *How to Spell What You Want to Be When You Grow Up*.

"I got the idea for my book," says Phil, "when my son wrote me from college saying he wanted to be a layer. I wrote him back and said, 'Son, that missing "w" just gave me a brilliant idea that will put you through law school!' The rest is history."

"I don't know," says Sally, toying with the ice in her drink. "I think he sounds like a real dumbass."

Martha and Sue are still huddled together on the couch. "Do you ever actually spend any money?" asks Sue. "It seems you recycle everything from tuna cans to blown-out boxers."

"Oh, sure I do," says Martha. "Last night, I threw a dinner party and served a flaming Spam entree that cost me $3.95. To compensate, I served the iced tea out of a Deli Cat container."

Here comes Uncle Herb, smiling and toying with his swizzle stick. I try to hide behind the rubber tree, but it's too late.

"Did I send you the one about the blonde who marries a man named Donald Duck?" he asks.

"No," I say. "But you did send me The Ten Commandments, The Beatitudes, and The Pledge of Allegiance, all rolled into one."

Martha taps me on the shoulder and whispers, "I never heard back from you on that friend thing I sent. You were supposed to reply if you were my true friend. And why don't you ever send the prayers back to me? Aren't you scared?"

"I've never learned the difference between delete and reply," I say.

"Well it's *your* soul," she says.

I don't know -- perhaps some meetings are better left in cyberspace. On the other hand, I may just go out and buy some invitations today. Better yet, get Martha to whip up a batch of freebies.

Anybody want to come to a party?

11. Fairest Fetus
of the Fair

 recently conducted an e-mail poll of pregnant women and the results were astounding.

They weren't worried about labor pains. They didn't mind the stretch marks. Hemorrhoids were tolerable, and the six-week waiting period was a real treat.

So what was the surprise?

Three of them already had their babies on a waiting list at Harvard. Five of them already had their baby's first birthday party planned. Ten of them had playgroups set up, complete with clowns and catered cupcakes, and twenty of them already had their baby girls signed up for beauty pageants.

One mother, Clarissa, was incensed about the current state of the beauty pageant circuit.

"It's just not fair," she wrote to me, "that their babies get to be in a pageant and mine doesn't. My baby already has a name, a designer wardrobe, and a headful of blond curls. The ultrasound technician said so! Marissa will be here in two more months, but by then the fall pageants will be over and she'll have to wait another year. I'm going to write President Bush. If he's going to allow stem cell research on our embryos, he should at least consider my request. I want my baby to be *Fairest Fetus of the Fair*. Isn't that reasonable? I mean, where is his sense of priority?"

Such a thought had never occurred to me, but I could see

her point. Who are we to say when discrimination begins? Is it conception? Quickening? Seven months? My heart went out to Clarissa and Marissa. I wanted to reach out to them, but I felt helpless. Then it hit me – I could form a chat discussion for these pregnant women so that they could vent their pageant frustrations in cyberspace. We gathered together online every night at nine o'clock. Although many of the women were in the midst of severe cravings, stuffing themselves with chocolate milkshakes and crackers, that didn't stop them from participating. Invisibility is one of the beauties of cyberspace.

Krystle from Alabama wrote, "My baby can't walk or talk yet, but she sure is purty. I think she would win *Fairest Fetus of the Fair*. Her big sister won first place last year in Tubby Toddler Miss, and her bigger sister placed second in Chubby Cherub Miss. It ain't fair."

Jane, an intellectual from Virginia, wrote, "I've waited years for this moment...put my body through torture to reach this point...and where did it land me? My timing has always been off! I'm sure Daphne would qualify for a full scholarship to Yale, if only they'd give her a chance. Why, she can already conduct music and pirouette. In five years they'll have a Fairest Fetus of the Fair, but my eggs will be too old. They're already 57!"

"Don't give up hope, girls," wrote Carla from Panama City. "I already have my nitrogen-cooled embryonic flask. We're a little ahead of y'all down here in Florida. My baby placed first in *Fairest Fetus of the Fair* last September. Now I'm going for Embryonic Fairest of the Fair. I think we got a good shot at it."

"She's right," wrote Darla from Daytona, "but the contests are rigged. We already have *Embryonic Fairest of the Fair* in Daytona but my little Sammy didn't even place. The ultrasound dude told me only experts could tell the sex of the child, but I think the judge knew he was a boy. I saw him snickering behind that crooked hand."

Before I could log out, all my pregnant cyber mates had packed their bags and moved to Florida. I hope they look out for alligators, sharks, and crooked judges.

12. Two A.M. Café

H ere in the midst of winter, I've gotten into a routine of curling up on the couch in front of the fire, dozing off early and waking up alone at 2 A.M. The fire has gone out and my husband and kids are asleep, so what do I do?

I enter the 2 A.M. Café, where a friend of mine is usually awake, too. We have similar hopes and dreams and sleep patterns, and when we wake up in the middle of the night, it comforts us to e-mail each other in the 2 A.M. Café, while the rest of the world sleeps on.

Lately we've been hoping and dreaming of snow. I write, "Down with Snowbird! Bad Snowbird! We got ZERO snow. I've been thinking, and I think Snowbird might be gay."

"I agree," she writes back. "But I've always thought that."

Sometimes we consider seeking help for our insomnia. She writes, "I do think the next time I go back to the doctor I will get something for sleep. But then again I do have to get up to go to the bathroom and I would hate to wet the bed."

And so we decide to keep the 2 A.M. Café open for now. Sometimes we talk about our husbands. I write, "Why doesn't anyone tell you that men do not peak at eighteen? It is a lie. The truth? They peak when they die. Their last words are, 'Wanna play?' Lately he's resorted to rhyme and alliteration. Left me a note with little red hearts that said, 'Sex at six?' 'Nibbles at nine?' 'Heaven at seven?'"

She writes, "Well you should be thankful he loves you so

much. And Valentine's Day is just around the corner."

I write, "I know, I know. And if I rock the boat too much I'll have to get up off the couch."

When I have my recurring dream about my teeth crumbling and falling out, I go to the 2 A.M. Café and that helps.

But sometimes the 2 A.M. Café is closed and I am forced to go elsewhere in Cyberspace. I check my junk mail and worry about the latest trend. Lately, the trash has come from the older crowd, and "Old and Nasty" and "Hot Grannies on Fire" are trying to reach me.

But they're not welcome in the 2 A.M. Café, so I delete them. Then I see an advertisement for Simple Green, "the finest non-toxic all-purpose cleaner in the world," and I wonder: Why is it green?

Outside my window tonight, the moon is shining on the shadows of the trees, and snow is swirling all around. The world can be a shimmering place at 2 A.M., and I e-mail my friend. "It's snowing!" I write. "Forget what I said about Snowbird!"

But my friend is sleeping and the 2 A.M. Café is closed for now. I check my e-mail and notice there's a new message from "A Word a Day," and I just have to find out what ahisma means. Ahisma: The principle of refraining from harming any living being. Hmmmm.

Tonight I am all alone at the 2 A.M. Café. But it will re-open when the wind blows hard and the floors creak in the night and our children drive back to college. Until then I will console myself with hopes and dreams of soft, billowy drifts of snow.

214

13. Lonesome Pink Dove

"Better to have it and not need it than need it and not have it."
—Captain Woodrow Call, Texas Ranger

L ove is a burning thing, and lately I've had a hard time making sense of it all. It's Oscar time again, but it's different this year. For best picture, The Academy of Motion Picture Arts and Sciences has nominated *Brokeback Mountain,* the story of two gay cowboys, while turning their noses at *Walk the Line,* the story of Johnny Cash's life. But here's the clincher: Larry McMurtry, writer of *Lonesome Dove,* wrote the screenplay for *Brokeback Mountain.*

For that reason alone, I may watch *Brokeback Mountain,* because *Lonesome Dove* is the best epic of all times, and McMurtry's talent is captivating. When people retire, they watch *Lonesome Dove* over and over and memorize the lines. True fans understand.

But I wonder what retired Texas Rangers Augustus McCrae and Captain Woodrow Call might have to say about *Brokeback Mountain.* Perhaps …

"It ain't right, Woodrow," says Gus. "Least I don't have to worry 'bout Lorie Darlin'."

"Well you always said a man who wouldn't cheat for a poke don't want one bad enough," says Call. "Come on now, we got work to do."

"Just wait'll Blue Duck gets a hold of 'em," says Gus, chewing on a blade of grass and smiling at the wide-open sky.

"Come on, Gus," says Call. "We got a herd of cattle to move. We can't afford to be thinking 'bout that sort of thing."

"You wouldn't never try to pull nothin' like that on me, would you Call?" asks Gus. "You ain't secretly turned that way, are you?"

"Hell, no," says Call. "Now get on up from there and shut your mouth. I don't want to hear such trash."

"You pull anything on me and I'll sic Pea Eye and Lippy on you," says Gus.

"You ever mention this again and I'll sic Blue Duck on you," says Call. "And you can forget about me hauling your dead butt all the way back to Lonesome Dove."

Yes, I may go see *Brokeback Mountain,* but I won't be watching the Academy Awards this year. Far as I'm concerned, anyone who disses Johnny Cash needs to be scalped by Blue Duck.

The Man in Black was not fully appreciated until his later years, and most recently, his death. Before he and June Carter Cash died, *Walk the Line* was underway, but initially, Columbia Pictures passed on the movie project. So did Sony, Universal, Focus Features, Paramount, and Warner Brothers.

What does Hollywood know, anyhow? They know how to make money, they know how to make a political statement, and they know how to reinvent arrogance and elitism.

Johnny Cash was and will forever be a legend known as "The Man in Black." The boys from *Brokeback Mountain* will merely be known as "The Men in Pink."

They better look out. Blue Duck's probably watching.

14. Dead Lip Pink

We all have moments when rude people catch us off guard and say something totally tacky. Typically, we are so taken aback that we can't spew out a clever comeback, but with practice, we can shoot those words right back into their mouths and all the way down to their crusty little toes.

Here are some possible scenarios and comebacks for that eternally rude question, "Why aren't you married?"

A rich old bitty from your church squeezes into her mink coat at the end of the service, and grasps your left hand. "Why aren't you married?" she asks. "A pretty thing like you needs a man, and if you wait much longer they'll all be taken."

A number of responses will suffice here, but I prefer the diversion tactic approach. Look to your left, then to your right, then stare directly at the nosy woman's throat with a puzzled look on your face. "What was that noise?" you ask. "It sounds like you swallowed a duck!"

Or you could stare at her lips for a good twenty seconds and say, "Have you seen the new shades of Venetio lipstick? They'd be perfect for you! They come in shades such as Old Lip Pink, Thin Lip Pink and Dead Lip Pink."

And then there's the age-old question, "Now *when* is your baby due?" that is also asked by Dead Lip Pink, five months after you have given birth to a darling baby girl named Jolene.

Here, the shock approach works best, and can sometimes invoke chest pains in the rude inquirer.

Let's say you are at Speedy Mart and Dead Lip Pink asks, "Now *when* is your baby due? It seems like you've been expecting for five years!"

"Have you not heard?" you ask incredibly. "Why, I was even on "The Today Show" last week!" At this point you will move close to Dead Lip Pink, and with great anticipation and excitement in your eyes you will say, "I have a three-headed alien growing inside of me, and my doctor has advised me to wait until it bursts out of my stomach all by itself! Oh, I think I feel it coming right now! I can feel its little claws scratching on my spleen!"

Perhaps the universal question that we have been asked is, "Have you gained weight?"

This scenario creates the perfect opportunity to invoke perpetual shame and guilt into the tarnished soul of the inquirer, who coincidentally is Dead Lip Pink.

Again, you are at Speedy Mart, out by the gas pumps when Dead Lip Pink asks, "Have you gained weight?"

You stare at her, obviously hurt, then throw yourself down on the ground and writhe around, screaming and flopping and hissing.

Dead Lip Pink will adjust her mink coat and look around to see if anyone is watching. "Good Lord, she says, "get up from there! Somebody will see you!"

You look up at her with pleading eyes and say, "After fifteen months of Slim Fast, 5,000 sensible meals, and a 100-pound weight loss, you ask me if I have gained weight? What kind of a person are you?"

Dead Lip Pink will try to console you in a hushed manner, ever conscious that someone may be watching. It's bad enough that's she's at Speedy Mart, but that's the only place she can stash up on her secret pork rinds. "Get up!" she whispers. "Get up right now!"

"This is it," you say, reaching up for the gasoline nozzle. "I am going to drink this gasoline, although I can't afford to pay for it, all because you asked me if I had gained weight. I have given up, and when St. Peter greets me at The Pearly Gates I am going to tell him that it's all your fault!"

Although I have not actually tried any of these approaches, I look forward to the opportunity.

15. Termite Man vs. Refrigerator Repairman

On this day and age, it is hard to get anyone to do repair work on time. So imagine my surprise when I arrived home from work the other day and found both the termite man and the refrigerator repairman in my kitchen. The refrigerator repairman was already hard at work, squatted down on the floor unscrewing the bottom of my refrigerator, while the termite man held a clipboard with contract in hand, wearing a big smile on his face.

I am leery of smiling men holding clipboards, yet they never seem to notice my skepticism unless my husband is with me. When my husband is with me, they tend to shut up and frown and get down to business, but I have figured out how to get them to this point on my own, in the absence of my husband, simply by telling them two things: "No," and "That's all I want to hear." Sometimes it is necessary to repeat these two phrases over and over, but eventually the men will stop smiling, pack up their clipboards and leave with contract unsigned.

I respected the refrigerator repairman from the start because he was halfway through the job, positioning himself in various degrees of discomfort, and he was wearing suspenders. Also, he confirmed my suspicions that when men don't know the answers, they make something up.

"When I talked to the repairman on the 800 number," I

220

said, "he told me the little computer inside my refrigerator was torn up and that was why it had suddenly defrosted all by itself, although it was only two years old."

The man peeped out from underneath my refrigerator and said, "You don't have a computer inside this thing," then proceeded to explain in great detail why the refrigerator had defrosted all by itself.

The termite man, upon hearing such logic, panicked and began his spiel. "Lady," he said, "your other termite company has gone out of business and we operate a little differently. You see, we use much stronger, safer chemicals than they did – chemicals that literally nuke a termite to shreds."

Southern men don't call women "Lady," and I was instantly repelled. "How much?" I asked.

Big toothy grin. "We'll get to that in a minute," he said. "First, I want to tell you something you probably don't know about termites. I don't mean to be graphic or anything, but termites regurgitate everything they eat and then regurgitate it all over again. They're very tenacious, and that is why we have to nuke them."

"Shut up," I said.

"You really can't afford not to sign this contract," he continued. "It may sound like a lot more than you were paying before, but in the long run it's much cheaper. We can guarantee a termite will never enter these premises again."

Meanwhile, the refrigerator repairman was almost finished with his job, and had begun telling me about the old house he grew up in, and how it was once owned by a mortician. I was fascinated by this tale of finding bones in the cellar and such, and the termite repairman was becoming desperate.

"Lady," he said, "I'll give you one month free. After that,

I'll be back for you to sign your contract – you won't regret it."

"No," I said. "There's no way $750 a year can be cheaper than the $50 a year we were paying. That is ridiculous, and that's all I want to hear."

He drove away in defeat, on to his next prospect, and I felt no guilt. After all, he was a grown man and I was a grown woman, both of us making adult choices in our lives.

It's the little things. He never should have called me "Lady."

16. Tootsie Roll Pop

He was all the way down to the chocolate. "When do you bite into a Tootsie Roll Pop?" asked my husband.

"Real soon," I said. "I always wonder how it would be to reach that chewy gooey middle, but then I'll take the fatal chomp after the first lick or two. I risk it all – chipping of teeth and destruction of dental work – possible decay of intact teeth. I'm like a hog on a corn cob. You got a problem with that?"

"No. It's just the way you are and I accept that.'

My husband is mature and this is good. Sometimes it is best to reach the heart of a matter in its own time, rather than stripping it down to the middle in a two-second fatal chomp.

Freud said, "Sometimes a cigar is just a cigar."

I say, "Sometimes a Tootsie Roll Pop is just a Tootsie Roll Pop. And sometimes it's not."

You can tell a lot about a person by the way they eat a Tootsie Roll Pop, the way they treat children and animals, and the way they act when they think on one is looking.

I am impatient and impulsive and my husband is patient and calm. Our traits complement each other so well that I can inhale a whole bag of Tootsie Roll Pops in the same amount of time he has reached the epicenter of one, and each of us is happy. Neither method is better but each route has its price.

Our dentist looks inside my mouth and plans ski trips to Aspen. He looks inside my husband's mouth and sees a Big Mac and fries.

The question is, "Is it worth it?"

The answer is yes.

One must always weigh the pros and cons, even in small matters such as Tootsie Roll Pops. For Tootsie Roll Pops are not small matters, because it isn't about the Tootsie Roll Pop at all. It's about life.

We all chart our courses and face the music. It may reach a sweet crescendo in record time, leaving you with nothing but a wet white stick to gnaw on, wondering what's next in your future. Or, the music may be a long-lasting harmony that leaves you with the satisfaction of knowing you listened well.

It's all very personal. I happen to like the rush of the red Tootsie Roll Pop crunch, mixed with the chocolate goo and the possible crumbling of teeth. The wait to the chocolate core might kill me because it is not my nature and that's OK. And while I do realize patience is a virtue, relaxation and peace do not come easy for me. Yoga is not in my future.

My favorite form of exercise and relaxation is hanging upside-down in my grandparent's maple tree which has been long-replaced by a lucrative technology business.

But the income it produces will never match the profit I gained from the land it sits on and the people who dwelled there. As Joni Mitchell put it, "They paved Paradise and put up a parking lot."

But what's all this talk of Tootsie Roll Pops and maple trees and pleasure versus patience? And can Paradise truly be paved? I think not. For parking lots can be replaced by memories of lf lazy days and innocence ... when we hung upside-down in our grandparents' maple trees with a big cherry Tootsie Roll Pop sticking out of our mouths.

To chomp or not to chomp?

That is the question.

Printed in the United States
92506LV00001B/127-225/A